CHEYENNE SATURDAY

Empty-Grave
Extended Edition

by
Richard Jessup

Empty-Grave
Publishing

Dear Reader,

As I was reading *Cheyenne Saturday* I found myself wondering about the "railhead" setting. The information I found may be of interest to other readers so I'm releasing this book as an Extended Edition and including a brief photo history of the Transcontinental Railroad. Enjoy!

The rest of Jessup's work will be released over time and my intention is to have just about everything he wrote back in print by 2015. Project information and updates are available at www.RichardJessup.com.

A.Nicolai
Empty-Grave Publishing

empty-grave.com - website

facebook.com/pages/empty-grave-publishing/114806311932977 - facebook

twitter.com/emptygravepub - twitter

feedback@empty-grave.com - comments, concerns, contact

Contents

Chapter One

THE JUNE SUN climbed quickly above the rim of the Nebraska plains and began drawing off the morning freshness of the grass. The railhead was now west of the North Platte River and with the first streaks of dawn, massive, burly Irishmen began moving out of their tents to stand before the flaps and stare out into the endless plains. In the distance, those farthest to the west could see the unhurried movements of black-brown buffalo grazing contentedly. And beyond the buffalo, they could see the markers of the surveyors where rails would be laid by nightfall.

The railhead began to stir itself awake. Voices of lean and hungry men broke the air. There were men wearing faded uniform trousers of both Confederate and Union Armies, with accents from a dozen regions and broken English from as many countries. And now, in the fullness of the chill morning, buckos, gang bosses, ex-sergeants and ex-officers moved among the sea of tents whipping their work gangs into haste. And the men who labored on the Union Pacific Railroad for seventy dollars a month whipped back at their buckos, often good-naturedly, often, too, with temper. They were not all ex-soldiers, obeying commands with the dispatch of army discipline. There were malingerers too, surly men who gambled and drank in the grog tents by night and sloughed their jobs during the day, whisky sweat drenching them under the Nebraska sun. But good-tempered or foul, they were wary, all of them, and alive to danger.

Danger on the railhead of the Union Pacific came any way at all. From the serpent-like slash of an enraged

Confederate's knife; the sly, unwarned blow of a drunken Irishman; the dart of a rattlesnake; the crash of a rail on a leg, leaving an injured man to die of gangrene far from home on the hot grassy plains. But more dreaded than these dangers, or the civilized threats encountered in Jeremy Watson's grog tents, from his women or his gambling tables, were the swift, brutal attacks of the Indians.

As the men grumbled and stretched their way into the cook tents for breakfast, Liam Kelly, six feet four inches and two hundred seventy pounds of Black Irishman, emerged from his tent. Thoughtfully, his eyes traveled the length of the plain's horizon, stopping momentarily on the herd of grazing buffalo, and then skipping to a low, swollen rise some twenty miles out ahead. His eyes rested on the hump while he bit into his first chew of tobacco of the day. He would use up five plugs before the sun went down.

"Slocum, lad," Kelly said to a young man passing him, "did the surveyors and graders all get back to camp last night?"

Slocum followed Kelly's gaze to the distant rise. "You thinkin' Goose Face out behind that hillock, Mr. Kelly?" he asked. He wore threadbare Confederate-gray trousers stuffed into the top of Texas boots.

"If he isn't, lad, I'll be more worried than I am, wondering where the bloody bastard might hit us next." Kelly shifted his tobacco cud to his other cheek, lodged it snugly behind his teeth, and spat neatly and accurately. "He's a clever bugger, Slocum, and he knows that today is Saturday—when the Johnny-Jacks will be drinkin' and carousin' in the grog tents with their pay."

"Well, Mr. Kelly," Slocum said, dropping easily to his haunches and sucking on a blade of grass, "seein' how this is war — fer him it's war leastways — I reckon I'd do the same thing. Hit us when we wasn't expectin' it." He nodded. "I never learned much else but fightin' in the conflict between the states, but I learned that. Hit 'em when they don't expect it."

Slocum, who was hardly more than twenty-one, twisted around. "I don't see Jake's hoss," he said thoughtfully, "so I guess he ain't in from scoutin'."

Kelly grunted. "I'll send Little out. Even if the graders and surveyors did come back, I don't like it. Now you get down to the grog tents and rush Little back here. Bring him to the general's office, and I want him sober, lad. If he's drunk, soak his head in a bucket of brine." He squinted toward the rise. "If Goose Face is out there, I want to know about it. And I want to know how many of them black-hearted braves he's got with him, and just what his position is."

* * *

His stomach pressing tightly against his snugly cinched belt after a breakfast of bacon, beans, biscuits and coffee, Kelly turned to the rails.

His eyes glowed with pleasure as he toured the gangs, whipped to more and more speed by the hawking buckos. A gang of twenty, well forward of the rest, graded the rise and filled in the hammock, lashed by the guttural tongue of ex-Sergeant Otto Pottsman, who had ridden with Sheridan. Behind them, three gangs received the ties from other gangs who hauled the heavy gear from wagons and carts. The drivers of the supply wagons whipped their horses furiously, their carts bouncing on the rough open plains in a mad dash back to the supply train farther up the line. Jehu was the name given to the wagon drivers, after the Biblical

9

king who raced his horses to death. Since most of the drivers were young boys, they were proud of the title.

Further back, more gangs slid rails from carts and dropped them deftly into place, working in swift rhythm. Then came the gaugers and the mallet men to tap the rails into position before the spikes were driven home in three perfectly-timed swings. There were ten spikes to the rail, four hundred rails to the mile, and the men had been known to lay eight miles of track in a working day.

Liam Kelly was too simple a man to characterize his love for railroad building as a dedication. He would have laughed in the man's face should one dare propose he was anything but a black-hearted Irish rail pusher—one who would drive, swear, plead, threaten, bluff, fight or kill to get the rails down. Kelly, who had seen his father push rails up and down the thin spine of the British Islands as a boy, and who himself had bucked the Cumberland Mountains when hardly out of his teens, ramming the rails westward for the Baltimore and Ohio, found happiness only when he could hear the incessant ripples of hammer strokes driving the spikes down and tying the rails to the earth forever.

Throughout the war Kelly had kept troops, supplies and munitions moving on the Pennsylvania with his unlimited strength, knowledge of railroads and uncanny knack for getting more out of men than they thought was in them. As a bucko in charge of a repair gang, Liam Kelly had more than once kept rolling stock flowing across the rails when raiders or Southern sympathizers wrecked terminal points, ripped up track and blew up trestles. Kelly had no side in the war. He worked for the railroad and would have thrown his strength to the Confederacy just as easily if he had been on the other side of the Mason-Dixon line when the first shot was fired on Fort Sumter.

The men worked well and freshly today, Kelly thought. Well, why shouldn't they? He turned to look down the thread of track that was all but hidden by muleskinners pulling in the fresh cross-ties and black, smoking iron men bringing up fresh rails, food, and other provisions. On either side of the double railing, a city of tents, all shapes, sizes and colors, sprawled. And all of it pointed, like the razor-sharp head of a Cheyenne arrow, to the rail-head where the Johnny-Jacks laid rail.

The men worked well, Kelly knew, because it was Saturday, and payday. He wondered if the pay train would be on time, or would Goose Face know about that too and waylay it? No, he thought, not with a full detachment of Union soldiers aboard.

The pay train would not bring only money for his Johnny-Jacks, Kelly thought morosely, walking swiftly towards the general's big tent. There would be more whisky for Watson's tents, more raffish women, more gun-slinging drifters, and always—always—rails, ties and equipment. And there would be the letters and boxes that kept the men from being lost in a sea of grass, buffalo meat and Indians.

Cheyenne Indians, Kelly grunted.

There would be new men on the train, too, replacements for those who had died, or ducked out on their contracts, or been killed in grog-tent brawls—untrained workers who would hold up the others until they caught the driving rhythm of the railhead that was linking two oceans.

Kelly stood outside the general's tent and looked at his watch, an old, gold Ever-Scott Hyland his father had given him. The pay train was due in half an hour, at six-thirty A.M. He nodded to the soldier on guard outside the

11

general's tent, and entered, leaving behind the anvil chorus of the railhead pushing for the Continental Divide.

* * *

"The general is tied up, Kelly," the young ex-major said amiably. "Can I help you?"

Kelly hesitated. "I kinda wanted to talk to him personal, Major."

Billy Brighton, graduate engineer, who had served with the general during the Civil War, tapped his lips thoughtfully with a pencil. The general personally had picked Kelly to be his troubleshooter when red tape and the character of the general's position would not allow him to handle things himself. Kelly was the man the general sent back to Omaha to find out why there was a delay in getting the Johnny-Jacks' mail to them. Six-feet-four-inch Kelly was the roving bucko who quelled riots and gang fights when feuding over the late war broke out among the laborers; Kelly was the man who beat four hard, tough muleskinners with his bare hands for threatening to dump their load of ties into the North Platte if they didn't get double wages. When the Johnny-Jacks were too hung over from their bouts in the grog tents to go to work Monday morning, it was Kelly who got them up on their feet and out to push rails.

A good man for his job, wise in the ways of railhead camps, Kelly knew when to be gentle and when to be rough. And Kelly also knew how to read the signs that foretold trouble. Anything, anything at all that would delay the Johnny-Jacks for three hours from laying rails was bucko Liam Kelly's job to fix. And if he could ward trouble off, Kelly answered only to the general as to his methods.

"It's Goose Face, Major," Kelly said. "There were rumors in camp last night."

"Goose Face!" Brighton looked grim. "The graders—the surveyors—they didn't get back to camp last night. That must be the reason."

Kelly's jaw set hard on his tobacco cud. "That settles it, Major, I have to see the general." He pushed past Brighton and through another corridor of tenting on into a larger tent. The general was talking to three men in Eastern clothes. He looked up.

"What is it, Kelly?"

"Goose Face, sir. And the graders and surveyors haven't gotten back to camp yet."

"Have you any specific information?"

"No, General, just suspicions."

The general stood up. "What about the scouts?"

"Jake didn't get back either, sir. I've sent for Little."

The three Easterners listened to the exchange between the general and the big, rough-looking man who could barge in unannounced. "Who is Goose Face?" one of them asked the general.

"One of Black Kettle's renegades," the general said.

"Who the hell is Black Kettle?" asked another of the Easterners.

"Congressman," the general said heavily, "if anybody should know who Black Kettle is, you should."

"See here—" the man protested.

The general waved a hand to indicate that he had not intended to be rude. "Black Kettle, gentlemen, is chief of the Cheyenne."

"But we are at peace with the Cheyenne."

"Not," said Kelly heavily, "since the massacre at Sandy Creek, Colorado, back in '64."

"Sandy Creek, Colorado? Massacre?" one of the three said. "What's that?"

"The United States Government had a peace agreement with the Cheyenne. In 1864 Union soldiers swooped down and killed every man, woman and child in a Cheyenne village on Sandy Creek," the general said bitterly. "Black Kettle swore vengeance."

"That's Black Kettle," one of the men said, "but who is Goose Face?"

"Goose Face, gentlemen," Kelly said, and spat onto the grassy floor of the tent, "is supposed to be the lone survivor of Sandy Creek. He was only a kid of fifteen at the time."

"A soldier's bayonet," the general interrupted, "slashed the boy's face. He was left for dead. But he lived," the general added heavily, "and there are a lot of settlers, Johnny-Jacks, women and children who would be alive today if he hadn't. He took a blood oath, or so the story goes."

"I believe it, General," Kelly said.

"I do too, Kelly." The general nodded. "The boy's wounds healed but left him horribly disfigured. The injuries to his chin and nose make him resemble a goose."

Kelly took up the narrative. "Since Black Kettle has declared war on all whites, Goose Face, a bitter lad of eighteen now, has gathered around himself a band of

14

about a hundred renegades—Cheyenne, some Sioux and any others who will swear death to the white man."

"Why hasn't something been done about him?" demanded one of the congressmen.

The General answered patiently: "We're building a railroad, Congressman—not fighting Indians. Goose Face is—though only eighteen—a full-grown man in warfare. He's cunning and ruthless. Very few men have ever seen him, and the story goes that he paints his face into a mask trying to cover his disfigurements. I've heard that he has killed men of his own who looked at him too long, or laughed."

"And you think he's near here?" one of the congressmen demanded. He turned to Kelly. "You think he might attack?"

"I don't ever think, mister," Kelly said without expression. "I can't answer your question until I know."

"When Little returns from his patrol, inform me immediately if Goose Face is in the area," the general said to Kelly, on a note of dismissal.

Outside the tent, Kelly snorted in annoyance at the dandified Easterners, even if they were congressmen. If they wanted to visit the railhead, Kelly grumbled to himself, they shouldn't mess their britches at the mention of a possible Indian attack. But Kelly, in his heart of hearts, didn't really blame the men from the East. There were tough Micks and ex-Confeds who thought twice before they dismissed the possibility of an Indian raid. And there wasn't a man in camp who hadn't heard about Goose Face's ruthlessness.

Kelly looked around for Slocum and Little. Not seeing either of them, he started off toward Watson's grog tents.

15

Kelly didn't mind a Johnny-Jack throwing his money away in poker games, or on women or grog, but he hated the manner of men who inevitably dealt in such services. And Jeremy Watson was as bad a man in that regard as Kelly had ever run up against. More than once the big Irish bucko had gone into the main saloon tent to pull Johnny-Jacks out by the neck and send them scurrying for the railhead. Watson would grin and say, "It's not my fault if they can't hold their liquor, Kelly." When a railman lost heavily at poker, and complained, Watson's gang of toughs would soon put an end to any bellyaching. So far Kelly had managed to stay shy of an open conflict with Watson, though he had been itching for one for months now. If a man couldn't hold onto his pay after working so hard for it, Kelly reasoned, then he deserved to lose it. But when a man was beaten so badly that he missed days and weeks on the rails, or perhaps even had to go back East, then Liam Kelly was involved. It took too long to get new recruits for the railhead, and that meant delay, and where there was delay it was Kelly's job to put an end to it.

It would have been simple for him to have the general order Watson and his women away, but the men working the rails wouldn't have stood for it. Isolated out here in these great, sandy plains, they had to have someplace to blow off a little steam.

He had gotten no more than twenty feet from the general's tent when he heard the howl and roar of the pay train. The railhead encampment greeted it with hoarse Irish curses and rebel yells. Tonight, Kelly thought wearily, the women in Watson's tents would get a big play, as would the gambling tables and the whisky crocks.

He turned in his tracks and went to meet the train and the new labor gangs from the East. And there was a little hope in his eye that a thick stack of letters would be on the train from Dublin and his Kathleen.

* * *

The detachment of armed guards had escorted the money boxes to the pay tent and gangs worked and sweated under the urgings of their buckos to unload the rails and new equipment. To one side, nearly a dozen newly arrived painted tarts joked with the men while waiting to be transported to Watson's tents. The mail had been taken off and carried to the general's office to be sorted and, with the mail, a column of engineers had marched off to be introduced to the general.

Further to one side, a group of nearly fifty raw labor recruits in ill-fitting city clothes threw nervous, excited glances over the sprawling tent city. It was to this group that Kelly attended.

"You've sold your souls into hell, lads," he bawled. "From here until the rail is down and tied to the earth at the Pacific shore, you're Johnny-Jacks! And you work until you break your backs!"

The men grinned awkwardly at each other. "We're building a railroad, lads, and we've come a hell of a long way without you, and I reckon we'll make it if you decide you can't take it. You're here to work and work you will, and I'm the bucko that can see there'll be plenty of it for you. We do one thing, and one thing only: we lay the rails down, lads, thataway—" Kelly turned and pointed toward the west. "Now you're to work in gangs and you've got a boss—a bucko who knows you haven't had experience, so he'll be patient with you—for one hour! Then you start working. All right, McCoy, call out your gang!"

A thin, deathlike figure in faded homespun trousers, battered hat and Confederate boots stepped forward and began reading off names.

The men fell out into a group, and a second bucko stepped up to collect his gang. Kelly stood to one side looking them over as their names were called, by and large quite pleased with the size of most of them. His eye fell upon one lean, bony-faced new arrival sitting on a Texas saddle, wearing Texas boots and hat. The man appeared to be ignoring the buckos forming up their gangs.

The man got up slowly and Kelly was surprised to see he was as tall as he himself was, though less bulky and given to the leanness and stringy muscles of Texans. Then Kelly saw the heavy black Colt anchored in a holster slung low and tied down to the thigh. Picking up the saddle, the man turned from the other laborers and started to walk away.

"Just a minute, lad," Kelly said. "Your name's not been called yet. You'll get lost if you don't know your gang."

The tall man turned slowly, his voice gentle, his eyes steady on Kelly's face. "I don't reckon he's going to call my name."

"Didn't you come out here to work on the Union Pacific?"

"No," the man said, "I didn't. But if you'll tell me where I can find Jeremy Watson's place, I'd be much obliged."

Kelly snorted. "Another worthless drifter come to scavenge around the railhead while honest men labor." Kelly spat a stream of tobacco juice in disgust. "Watson's place, eh! You'll find that easy enough. Just follow the worst stink in camp and you'll be home. That'll be Jeremy Watson's."

18

"I've heard stories about big Irish mouths but I never believed them, up to now," the tall man said.

Kelly's head snapped up as if on a string. "And I've heard that gunslingers quiver in their own spit when they unbuckle their irons and drop them in the dust."

Smiling tightly, the bony-faced man lowered the saddle to the ground and unbuckled his heavy gunbelt. His eyes never leaving Kelly's face, he unleashed the tie-down of the holster.

Men stopped in their labor to watch as the two moved toward each other. It was not often that Kelly found anyone who would argue on a second breath with him, but from the size of the tall Texan and his ham-like fists, there were Johnny-Jacks in the crowd who thought they were going to see Kelly meet his match.

A circle had been made and the onlookers began to chant to mix it up. Kelly advanced, alert and ready. The Texan waited for him, arms hanging loosely at his sides.

"Mr. Kelly!" a voice yelled from the circle of men. A boy of fourteen slithered through. "Mr. Kelly, the general wants to see you right away. He said right away!"

"Boy!" Kelly roared. "Can't you see I'm about to mix with this no-good son of a bitch? Now git outa here!"

"But, Mr. Kelly! The general said right away!"

The Texan straightened up and backed off. "I wouldn't want you to lose your job, Irishman. You better hop to it before you get slapped on the wrist for neglect of duty."

Kelly's face went crimson. He spat out his cud. "God damn it! Come on, come on and fight! Hang the general!"

But the Texan was smiling openly now, and so were many of those in the circle. "Naw, I ain't going to fight

19

you. You come look me up after you've polished the general's brass."

Kelly nearly exploded. "You promise me that!" he demanded. "You give me your word as a worthless skunk you won't run out until we meet—man to man— you promise?"

"I promise." the Texan said, buckling on his gunbelt. "You'll find me at Jeremy Watson's." And then with a twinkle in his eyes, the tall Texan looked down at the boy. "Son are you sure the general sent you after this Irishman?"

Kelly stamped with rage and disgust. Then he turned and pushed through the laughing men. "Boy," he said and bit down on a fresh chew of tobacco. "If'n the general don't want me as bad as you say, I'm goin' to tan your sittin' place."

"Oh, he wants you all right, Mr. Kelly. There's an Injun fighter in buckskin wanting to see you," the boy replied, trotting alongside him. "And Mr. Kelly, sir."

"Yeah?"

"This Injun fighter—is a woman."

* * *

Kelly stared at Liza Reeves and couldn't help but wrinkle his nose. "You're Jake's brother—" Kelly said. "I mean, Jake's your sister—"

"You don't talk good, do you mister?" Liza Reeves said tartly.

"I—I'm sorry, ma'am," Kelly said, searching her person with his eyes and taking in her worn buckskin trousers and buckskin blouse with half the fringe gone, used long ago to lace something or other together. She wore a battered Texas hat and her jet-black hair had been pulled

20

back over her ears to hang in a tangled mat on the nape of her neck. Her face was burned nearly brown-red from the plains' sun and the color accentuated the flashing blue eyes. Her teeth were white and strong. Kelly figured she couldn't be more than twenty-two or -three. And even underneath the grime and the buckskin, he could see there was a strong, hard body. A very womanly body. And Kelly thought, looking at her, wanting desperately to hold his nose, if she didn't smell so bad she might even be pretty. He glanced toward Billy Brighton, who stood at a safe and respectful distance, holding the tent flap open for fresh air. No wonder the general said hurry!

Kelly snorted. "Well, ma'am, Jake ain't come back from his night's scouting yet."

"Perhaps," Brighton added quickly, "the lady would like to freshen up a bit. She would be welcome to use my quarters."

Liza Reeves stood up. "I reckon I could do with a wash," she said, hefting a heavy rifle and easing the weight of her Colt. "I feel like I'm carryin' ten ton of the dust with me from the ride down from west of the badlands."

Brighton and Kelly looked at each other. "You rode down from the badlands—*alone?*" Kelly gasped.

"Why, sure," Liza said easily. "When you figure Jake will skiddle into camp?"

Kelly forgot about how Liza Reeves smelled and impulsively grabbed her by the shoulders. "Then you came down through—"

"Take your hands off me or I'll blow your guts out," she said, and Kelly felt the press of her gun in his stomach. He dropped his hands to his sides and stepped back.

"No offense, ma'am, I just got excited."

Billy Brighton grinned widely.

"Well, don't go 'round gettin' excited with me," Liza said in a steely voice. "Now, what was you askin'?"

"How did you come down? What route did you take to get here?"

"I just tramped down the Powder River as far as the Belle Fourche, then lit straight down to the North Platte and followed it on in," Liza said.

"Did you meet any Cheyenne?"

"Are you teched in the head, mister? Sure I met Cheyenne, and some Crow huntin' parties and Arapaho."

"Did you meet any large groups of Cheyenne?"

"You don't meet large groups of Cheyenne these days, mister," Liza Reeves said. "You stay downwind from 'em, or ain't you heard of Sandy Creek yet and how Black Kettle feels about it?"

"I didn't mean that. I meant—"

"Then say what you mean. I'll swear, you don't sound right."

"We heard Goose Face was close by."

"I didn't see him," Liza said seriously. "You think he's around here?" Her eyes flashed, and then she broke out into a dazzling grin. "Well, if he is, ol' Jake will know about it. As for me, I didn't see that child."

Words failed Kelly.

Liza hefted her rifle. "All right, now that you finished questionin' me" —she turned to Billy Brighton— "this good-lookin' fellow can show me where I can wash some."

"I'd be delighted, ma'am," Billy Brighton said. "If you'd just follow me." And he hurried out of the tent to keep well ahead of Liza Reeves.

"You tell ol' Jake his sis is here if he comes in 'fore I get back," she said to Kelly.

"Yes'um, I'll tell him."

She flashed the big Irishman a grin. "I left my horse with a boy the general sent for you. Is he trustin'?"

"He'll take good care of your horse, ma'am," Kelly said and turned away quickly to the flap, and fresh air.

* * *

It was close to seven in the morning when Kelly moved through the camp. Up ahead, Watson's tent with the ten-foot flaps opening into the lantern-lit interior was already beginning to rouse itself and serve whisky to shaking old men and drunkards.

Simpson and Garrity, two of Watson's gang, sat on either side of the huge opening, their Colts low and ready, and watched Kelly approach.

"Morning, Kelly," Simpson, the larger of the two, said, a small grin forming on his thin lips.

"How do, Kelly," Garrity said.

Kelly ignored them and marched into the tent. He stopped to let his eyes grow accustomed to the light and stared around, searching for Slocum and Little. In the middle of the tent were three rough wooden planks laid side by side and stretched across sawhorses in a rough circle. This was the bar, and behind it, on still other planks, was row after row of cheap whisky in bottles of every imaginable size and color. Red-eyed bartenders in undershirts had begun laying in the day's supply of drink in anticipation of the night's crowd. The grassy floor had been stomped into a mire for ten feet around the bar where the Johnny-Jacks had pushed and shoved their way to the front the night before. In one dark corner several men lay flat on their backs sleeping off heavy loads of grog. In another corner, wearing knee boots and gingham dresses and clustered around rough tables, the women sat on rawhide stools, waiting.

Slocum and Little were seated at a nearby table, and it was obvious that Little would not ride scout that day. His head lay peacefully on his arms and Slocum stood beside him, looking down uncertainly at the inert figure. He looked up at Kelly's approach, and relief passed over his face. The big Irishman moved down the side of the bar toward the table, unseen by Watson and the half-dozen of his men clustered together on the other side of the circle of rough planking.

"I see you kept your word, Irishman."

So intent was Kelly on the tableau of an unconscious Little and a hovering Slocum that he did not notice the tall Texan leaning against the bar. The Texan pushed forward and barred Kelly's way. "I reckon you want satisfaction now," he said. He was grinning good-naturedly and he began to unbuckle his gunbelt.

Kelly was staring absently at the slumped figure of Little, already thinking of what man he could send out as scout to relieve Jake Reeves and be depended on to bring an honest report. There wasn't a one. "Not now, Texas," he said gruffly. "I'm busy."

He pushed past the tall man, who looked after him with thoughtful eyes. "Can't you sober him up, Slocum?" Kelly said.

24

Slocum glanced at Watson and his men. "He ain't drunk, Mr. Kelly. He's been pistol-whipped."

Kelly jerked up. "Who done it?"

Slocum nodded in the direction of Watson.

"Get him over to the doctoring tent, lad," Kelly said grimly.

Slocum nodded and hefted Little over his shoulder. His boots sinking into the mud, he struggled past the tall Texan and out of the tent.

"Who did it?" Kelly demanded of Watson and his men. "Which one of you yellow-bellied scum was afraid to shoot—but beat that lad with his gun?"

"Hold on Kelly," Watson said harshly. "There was a little misunderstanding, and then your scout tried to pull a knife."

"Asa Little would never give a man a chance if he had pulled his knife," Kelly said. "And I said *if* he pulled his knife."

"Come on and have a drink, Kelly," Watson said with a shrug.

"Who whipped my scout!" Kelly roared. "Step out and whip me, if one of you dares to face up to a man!"

The men glanced at each other. Then one of them stepped out, a thick-set, wide man. "Kelly, I've had enough of your bellowing. I whipped your scout. Now what'n hell you think you going to do about it?"

Watson had moved a safe distance away. The Texan leaned at the bar, sipping his whisky and watching the scene.

Kelly moved in on the thick-set man and knocked him sprawling. "Get up!" he roared.

At a sign from Watson the other men circled Kelly, removed their guns, and reversed the butts. The big Irishman charged, his fist catching one man and knocking him cold. But as he moved, the others got behind and around him and began to hammer at his head.

The Texan finished his drink, removed his hat and stepped into the fray. He reached one man on the back of the head with his own gun-butt, and was slugged in return by one of Watson's men. Kelly slammed a man back against the planking, and tore down a whole section. The Texan landed heavily against the inner bar, and bottles and crocks of whisky fell with a crash. He bulled his way back to where three Watson men were hammering at Kelly and, in turn, began methodically chopping at the Watson men.

A reeling man fell hard against one of the thick tent poles and half the tent fell in on the fighters. The women began to scream, and when neither Kelly nor the Texan could find anyone to swing at, they scrambled out from underneath the canvas. They stood outside the stricken tent and looked over each other solemnly, sucking at their knuckles.

"I forgot my saddle and hat in the tent," the Texan said gravely.

He turned and scooped up one edge of the tent and disappeared.

Kelly waited. There were sudden loud smacking sounds, a crash of bottles and the heavy thud of a man going down. Then silence.

The edge of the tent was lifted and the Texan emerged with his saddle and his hat, replacing his Colt in its holster. Kelly's face was heavy with chagrin.

"I want you to know, I didn't ask you to help me!" Kelly said, "I could have handled those toughs without your help."

"I know you didn't ask me," the Texan said mildly.

"And it don't change anything between us," Kelly insisted.

"Not a thing," the Texan said agreeably. He dropped his saddle into the dust and began unbuckling his belt. "Now be all right?"

"No, I got work to do." Kelly said regretfully.

"All right, I'll be around somewhere, I reckon." The Texan picked up his saddle and began to walk off.

"Wait a minute!" Kelly called as he hurried to the man's side. "You told me you was working for Watson. How come you lit in against him?"

"I didn't say no such thing." The Texan said.

"You asked me how to get to Watson's."

"That's what I asked you."

"God damn it, man!" Kelly roared. "I ain't going to stand here and quibble with you—"

"Then don't."

"If you didn't come here to work for Watson, and you didn't come here to work on the railroad, what in hell did you come here for?"

"I don't figure that's any of your business, Irishman," the Texan said politely but firmly. "But it won't hurt none to tell you. You might know the man I'm after."

"Oh, are you lookin' for somebody who works in this camp?"

"That's right."

"Who?"

"He calls himself Lefty Hayes."

"Lefty Hayes!" Kelly said. "He works for Watson. He's Watson's right-hand man."

"That's what they told me down in Independence and in Omaha," the Texan said levelly.

"Whatcha want with him?"

"Goin' to kill him."

Kelly shook his head sadly. "Son," he said, "you're a big, strapping lad, and you've shown yourself to be fair-minded and capable with your fists, but Lefty Hayes is faster than a rattlesnake with that gun of his'n."

"I heard."

"Are you fast?"

"I ain't dead yet."

"No, you ain't, lad, but you might be if you try to kill Lefty Hayes."

"Well, one way or the other, I'm gonna try."

"I can't stand here talkin' to you. I've got work to do. You got anyplace special to go while you're waitin' for Lefty?"

"Nope."

"Walk with me over to the doctorin' tent while I see how my scout is farin'."

"All right," the Texan said.

"I could sure use a man like you." Kelly eyed the Texan. "It's a great thing, lad, to be part of buildin' a railroad—not just any railroad, but one that will build a strong country."

28

"Seein' as how I just spent nearly five years doin' everything I could to tear that country apart; I don't guess I got much interest." They moved through the tents.

"You wore the gray, eh, lad?" Kelly's voice was gentle. "I can't say that I blame you for feelin' bitter. It was a hard-fought war."

"I don't feel bitter," the Texan said simply. "I just ain't a railroad man."

"We have a lot of Confederate lads workin' side by side with their former Union foes."

"The war's over for me," the Texan said shortly. "Except for one little piece of unfinished business."

"Lefty?"

"That's right."

"I reckon we oughtta introduce ourselves, lad," Kelly said. "I'm Liam Kelly, bucko in charge."

"How do, Mr. Kelly. I'm Nathan Ellis."

The men shook hands. "Texas, eh?" Kelly said, indicating the boots and the hat.

"Texas," Ellis said.

Kelly scratched at his chin. "You wouldn't be one of those lads who sneaked supplies into the Confederacy under the noses of the Yankees, would you?"

Ellis grinned. "We did manage to get a few wagonsful of stuff to the boys."

Kelly grunted. Texas had sided with the South in the conflict, but had not been as actively engaged in actual fighting as the others, its role being principally the supply of men and material, much of it brought overland from the Pacific coast. It took hard, tough men to cart guns and ammunition nearly two thousand miles across the southern deserts, fighting Indians and raiders every step of the way. His estimation of Nathan Ellis rose another notch.

"I'll be right back, Ellis," Kelly said. He turned into the tent and dismissed the Texan from his mind, his attention now wholly focused on his problem. How badly was Asa Little injured, and could he ride scout to relieve Jake Reeves? And if he couldn't, who was there to replace him?

Even if he had to go himself, Kelly had to have information on the whereabouts and plans of the renegade Goose Face.

Chapter Two

GOOSE FACE didn't mind the stench of the buffalo dung he had so carefully smeared over his body to cover his own scent. Bent over and nearly on all fours beneath the weight of a bull buffalo's hide, complete with skull and horns, the young Cheyenne ignored the herd grazing around him and concentrated on the scene nearly twenty miles away across the plains. The railhead camp, with its city of tents and spirals of smoke from big campfires, delighted him.

He studied the scene with the eye of one well experienced in attack. It was useless to come up from across the plains and attack the white men head-on. They would be warned and ready for him, and he and his hundred followers would be wiped out in the first sally.

Though the young Indian did not understand much that motivated the white man, he had learned enough from the trader who had taken him in after the massacre of his village to know that this day, this night, was important to them. The greeting staged earlier by the white men for the iron horse confirmed his meager information that today was some sort of feast day for the men who broke trail for the smoking horse. He had learned from the scout taken during the night that it was Sad-a-day, and he remembered that the old trader never failed to drink whisky on Sad-a-day.

What bothered Goose Face as he moved through the herd of buffalo was the number of soldiers. He was torn between the pleasant dream of killing so many of the killers-of-his-people and the honest respect he had for them as fighters. These soldiers, the young Cheyenne knew, had

31

just finished fighting a war between themselves and there was nothing so dangerous as a brave who has learned the tricks of battle, and who does not flinch at death.

Now, even as Goose Face watched the railhead encampment, the spur of rails had inched closer to him and the herd of buffalo. Suddenly his eyes gleamed. He had his plan.

He turned and worked his way back through the herd to where he had hobbled his pony. He slung the buffalo hide to the ground and leaped on his swift broomtail stallion and trotted of in the direction of the rise that had caused Liam Kelly so much anxiety.

Behind him, the rails inched closer and closer. The buffalo closed in after him, nuzzling the deep plains grass and one another.

* * *

Goose Face's men lay in wait in the depth of a shallow gully that, during early spring, would run full and wide and empty into the North Platte, but was now dry and loamed with hard red dust. There was no shade, and the men sat cross-legged in the shadows of their broomtails and talked among themselves. To one side Jake Reeves lay sprawled in the sun, bound hand and foot and pegged spread-legged to the ground. No one watched him any more, for Jake had ceased to struggle during the night. The blood from a head wound, inflicted by Goose Face in extracting information, had long since clotted over and the spill had dried into the dust.

Farther up the draw, twenty or more of the ragged renegade band were grouped around a tall brave who was gesturing to the others and talking slowly. The circle of men listened to Singing Bird, a wandering Blackfoot who had been driven out of his village for theft, and did not respond to his tirade.

Some of them turned away without a word. Others followed, and when Singing Bird tried to make them listen, his eye caught sight of a pony standing above him on the edge of the dry bank.

Goose Face stared at the man below. "So," he said between his teeth, "you would have us sneak into the white man's camp and steal like the thief you are!"

Caught, Singing Bird tried to bluff his way out. "Many of us do not like attacking the white man."

"You do not like attacking the white man," Goose Face said, nudging his pony down the bank.

"I challenge any brave in my hatred of the long beards!" Singing Bird shouted.

"You sing like the bird and are named justly," Goose Face said angrily. "A vulture!" Moving swiftly, he slipped his knife into Singing Bird's stomach and, with the bone-handled hilt flat against the man's skin, twisted it.

Goose Face withdrew the knife, wiped it on the buck-skin trousers of the slain man and turned to face the emotionless stares of his men. More than half of them were Cheyenne who had been cut off from Black Kettle during raids. There were many Sioux, as many Pawnee and some Arapaho and Crow. All of them had tasted the treachery of the white man and were dedicated to his death, but all of them had not come to Goose Face to join forces against the long beards. Many of them, like Singing Bird, had been cast out of their villages for violating tribal taboos. But if they swore allegiance to Goose Face—who promised nothing but hardship and war in his sworn vengeance against the whites—the past crimes that brought them into the young renegade's party were forgotten. "Is there another who thinks he has enough coups in his lodge to challenge the will of Soft-and-Running-Deer?"

The Cheyenne leader did not know that the white man's name for him was Goose Face, and spoke his true name.

None of the men moved.

"The buffalo stand between us and the whites," Goose Face went on. "When the sun is here—" he pointed to the horizon where the sun would begin to sink—"and the long beards are beginning their Sad-a-day feast with much whisky, some of us will stampede the buffalo into their camp. And when the beasts have run them down, we will attack from there." He pointed east and beyond the railhead camp.

The older Cheyenne, who were not dishonored but were true Cheyenne who had been cut off from their people, agreed that Goose Face had devised a clever plan in using the buffalo.

Selecting a group of twenty of his best men, Goose Face planted a stick in the ground and drew a line some distance away. "When the shadow crosses this mark, you will start the buffalo toward the whites!" Goose Face spat the word out with contempt. "Then you will follow the beasts and slay the long beards."

Goose Face looked over his party. "Today we pay our revenge for the destruction of Soft-and-Running-Deer's people, for the day when the blood of squaws and little ones ran over by horses' hoofs!"

Instructing those who remained to kill the scout before they stampeded the buffalo, Goose Face mounted his pony and led his party far to the west, walking slowly to avoid dust trails and circling far to the north to bring up east of the railhead.

Those who were left in the draw posted sentinels down close to the buffalo herd to watch for other scouts who might come out from the railhead in search of the first. The remaining men sat in the shadows of their ponies and talked softly among themselves, recounting the days of their fathers' childhoods when there were no white men pushing across the plains, and the only danger was hunger and cold, and telling of the pleasures of forging north to the headwaters of the Missouri and raiding the Mandan for women.

* * *

"This man won't sit on a horse for six months," the doctor told Kelly. The big Irishman glanced down at the silent form of Asa Little, whose head was swathed in bandages.

"Thank you, Doctor," Kelly said and turned quickly from the tent.

"How's your man?" Ellis asked.

"Lucky to be alive," Kelly grunted. "Somebody oughtta string that Watson to one of his own tent poles."

"What's all the sweat about?"

"Goose Face," Kelly said heavily. "Our night scout didn't come in—neither did the surveyors or the engineers."

Ellis squinted into the middle distance where the buffalo grazed. "That youngun around here?"

"There were reports from the south by muleskinners bringin' up cross ties that some settlements had been hit by that youngun," Kelly said bitterly. "Only he's not a youngun, he's a cutthroat Cheyenne with a hatred in him that can be cut out only with a knife."

"I reckon you got a problem, Kelly," Ellis said, walking beside the bucko toward the general's tent. "Goose Face is one stubborn Injun."

"You ever have any trouble with him?"

"I seen him once. I was kickin' up dust along the Santa Fe trail headin' for Independence lookin' for this Lefty—me and a few other hardtails—when we rousted Goose Face and a party of about twenty from killing off a tradin' post."

"He's got more than twenty followin' him now. I hear it's closer to a hundred and twenty," Kelly said grimly.

"Well, you sure got a problem." The Texan shook his head, still squinting at the buffalo. "If he's got a hundred and twenty men—yes sir, Kelly—you got a problem."

"You eat yet, lad?"

"No, I ain't and I'm pretty hungry," Ellis said.

"I've got to see the general and tell him the situation. That's my tent over there," Kelly said, pointing. "There's a whucked-up Jehu hobblin' around on one foot and a cane that fixes for me. You tell him I said to feed you."

"Right kind of you, Kelly. Thank you," Ellis said courteously.

While Kelly strode off toward the general's tent, Ellis stepped over tent guys and dropped his saddle in front of a tent. A young boy of about eighteen, leaning on a makeshift crutch, grinned up at Ellis. "Mr. Kelly ain't here, mister."

"I know, boy," Ellis said amiably. "I been sent over to eat by the very man himself. You reckon you could rustle me some coffee, beans and bacon?"

"Sure," the boy replied.

"Where can I wash off some engine smoke? I been ridin' your damned railroad all night on an open flatcar."

The boy jerked a thumb around the side of the tent.

"How'd you hurt your foot?"

"Wagonload of rails spilled and I didn't jump quick enough," the boy replied with an infectious grin.

Ellis dug into his pocket and flipped a silver dollar toward him. "Hot coffee," Ellis said, "strong enough to bite back."

"Yes sir!"

Ellis moved around the side of the tent to a community washstand, consisting of a rough plank, several basins and a donkey-drawn cistern of water on high wheels.

A black-haired, buckskin-clad figure was bending over a basin swishing water and gurgling happily. Ellis stepped up and slapped the figure on the seat with a resounding whack. "Move over, hardtail," he said good-naturedly.

The figure whirled, black hair a tangled, dripping mess, hurled the basin of water into Ellis's face and shoved him off balance into a wallow of mud. While he was still spluttering, Ellis heard the unmistakable click of a Colt hammer pulled back.

"You make that kinda mistake again, mister," Liza Reeves said, finger on the trigger, "and I'll take your ears off one piece at a time."

Ellis could only stare at the apparition with the tangled, dripping hair.

To one side, Billy Brighton stepped out of his tent and offered Liza Reeves a towel. He looked at Ellis, still sprawled in the mud, and grinned. The tall Texan watched them walk away.

"Well I'll be damned!" he said.

"Whatcha doing down there, mister?" The crippled boy had moved to the washstand and was grinning broadly. "Your coffee's ready."

"I'm comin', boy, just give me time," Ellis said, shaking his head.

* * *

"The graders and survey engineers are back, Kelly," the general said. "They had gotten so far out, they decided to make camp last night. And Jake Reeves will probably show up, too. Jake's a damned good scout. It would take a lot more cunning than Goose Face possesses to get a good man like him." The general smiled. "Relax, Kelly. I heard the boys have already put down nearly two miles, and it isn't ten o'clock yet."

Kelly grunted. "I'd like to talk to them just the same."

The general grinned. "Go ahead."

Kelly left the big tent and, after a quick check around the railhead, headed for the survey tent.

"Did you see anything at all?" he demanded of the head of the survey party that had gone out two days before.

"Not a thing, Kelly," the man replied. "Last night we saw Jake makin' a fire about thirty miles west of the railhead."

Kelly frowned. "You saw Jake making a fire? Are you sure it was Jake?"

"We didn't go over and pass the time of day with him, Kelly," the man said. "But who else could it have been?"

"It could have been Goose Face and his party, that's who!" Kelly snapped. And then he apologized. "I'm sorry. I guess I'm gettin' to where I see Injuns behind every bush."

The survey engineer smiled thinly. "We penetrated nearly forty miles due west and didn't see so much as a rabbit."

Kelly stamped out of the tent and headed back for his own quarters.

"Saddle my horse, boy," he roared as he approached his tent.

"Goin' for a ride?" Ellis asked, sitting cross-legged on the ground, working on his fourth tin plate of beans. He watched Kelly strap on a heavy Colt and turn to his rifle.

"Seems like I'm the only one in this camp," Kelly said, "that sees any danger in Goose Face."

"Then you ain't got many bright people in your camp," Ellis said, chewing on his beans. "You goin' to ride out and take a look?"

"I am."

Ellis squinted. "You had an experience ridin' scout against Cheyenne?"

"I'm goin' out lookin' for Jake," Kelly said stubbornly.

"Didn't Jake get in yet?" a voice said in the tent opening. They spun around to see Liza Reeves standing in the light. "How come you ridin' out to look for ol' Jake?" she asked quietly. Her eyes took in the heavy awkwardness of Kelly's sagging Colt. "Ain't there no more scouts in this setup to go out? And what makes you think ol' Jake needs lookin' after?"

Kelly was checking his rifle, one of the new breech-loaders, and shoving cartridges into his pockets. "Ma'am, there're a few people in his camp that don't think much of my fears that that sly devil Goose Face is in the area, but I'll tell you straight out that I think he is. And with my scout Asa Little laid up in the doctoring tent with a busted head, somebody's got to go lookin' around to see where he is."

Liza Reeves appeared to see Ellis for the first time. "Whyn't you send him ? He looks like a trail rider."

"I don't work for the railroad, ma'am," Ellis said and continued to eat his beans.

"Where'bouts you think ol' Jake might be?" Liza Reeves asked.

"He was headin' for the big grass due west of here," Kelly said.

"Well, I might just ride along with you," Liza said decisively.

"No, you won't," Kelly said shortly. "You might be free to ride down from the Missouri badlands by yourself, but you're not—"

Nathan Ellis nearly choked on a mouthful of beans. "She came down from up north—*alone?*"

Liza Reeves glanced at Ellis with impatience. "Are you one of them that thinks a woman can't live without the help of a man?"

"No, ma'am," Ellis said. "I guess I made a mistake. I shoulda known that any woman that would walk around with her hair lookin' like yours, and wearin' buckskin and smellin' as bad as you do, wouldn't need a man— and had lost hopes of ever gettin' one."

40

Liza Reeves's face turned violently red. She hefted her rifle and spoke to Kelly. "What time you leavin'? You gotta give me time to get my horse."

"You're not goin' with me!"

"You don't think you're goin' to stop me, do you?"

Kelly looked at Ellis in dismay. Ellis grinned. "Might as well take her, Kelly. If your horse breaks a leg, she can carry you into camp on her back. Damned if she don't look strong enough."

"I knew you wouldn't fight me 'cause I'm a woman, but I wish—"

Liza Reeves didn't get a chance to finish here wish. A tremendous explosion rocked the air, followed by a second and then a third. The ground quivered under the shock and then, rising out of the deafening noise, came the shrieks and wails of injured men.

"Good God almighty!" Kelly roared and sprang to the opening of the tent, Nathan Ellis and Liza Reeves right behind him.

* * *

For two hundred yards along the sides of what had been Union Pacific track, tents and wagonloads of equipment had been blown over as if by a giant wind. And, instead of shining rails laid out in perfect alignment, there was a hole torn in the plains four feet deep and nearly fifty yards long. Whole lengths of track had been hurled three hundred feet and lay twisted and useless. Two sets of wheel trucks had been blown fifty yards. Cross ties had soared into the air and splinters were still raining down on the army of rescuers surging into the scorched field. Men lay on the ground by the score, some of them with the silence of death about them. Others crawled on all fours, blood streaming from their faces, eyes glazed with shock. And others screamed with pain and begged for relief.

"The powder car!" a Johnny-Jack shouted in explanation as Kelly fought his way to the center of the devastation. "Nobody knows how it happened!"

When the last of the flying, cross-tie splinters had settled to earth, Kelly took charge. His big voice roared orders to the Jehus to dump their wagon loads of ties and gear and haul the wounded to the medical tent. The furious young drivers lashed their horses mercilessly, bringing up their wagons where ready hands were picking up the injured.

Here and there the keening wail of an Irish lass rose to the big sky as a Johnny-Jack breathed his last. The dead were covered with blankets, and the ones in shock were held by strong hands as they fought against the fury of the nightmare.

Scenes of pity, bravery, and despair reached out and touched Nathan Ellis, who worked quickly, quietly and effectively helping the wounded. But the big Texan had seen too much death and suffering during the war to be, stricken, as had many of the men who recognized the whip of authority in his voice and responded, not knowing who he was or if he had such authority rightly.

And Liza Reeves worked swiftly and surely. At the first sight of the disaster, she had breathed silently to herself, "Bandages!" and had taken off through the tent community snatching sheets and towels and clean laundry from lines and ripping them into strips. Coolly she examined the men's wounds, and with nothing more than her frontier experience, decided whether they should be attended to at once in the medical tent or wrapped tightly in bandages to prevent bleeding while they waited until the more badly injured were cared for.

Kelly recruited a crew of two hundred men with shovels and picks, and another hundred with trace teams to haul away the heavier wreckage, and began at once to clear the disaster area. Digging and shoveling, the army of workers began filling in the gash torn into the plains, while another army moved in to repair the gap.

"How may dead?" Kelly asked Ellis when the Texan moved slowly through the tents back to the scene of the tragedy.

"Thirteen," Ellis said. "And seven not expected to make it longer'n tonight. There're about thirty-five that I can count who won't do any more railroadin'." He watched the feverish activity of the gangs repairing the tracks. "You don't lose much time, do you, Kelly?" His voice was a little tight.

"We're out here to build a railroad," Kelly said succinctly.

"It could just as easily've been me — or you — or anyone else that was standin' near that car when it blew up."

"I reckon," Ellis said.

"Did you see that gal workin' on the men?"

"I saw," Ellis said.

"Cool as a tinhorn gambler, she was, workin' with those men. Not may women in this camp coulda looked at the blown-out insides of a man, seein' what he ate for breakfast, and keep goin' without a flinch or a quiver."

Ellis nodded.

Both men turned to watch Liza Reeves walk past them with her arm around a woman who had lost a husband and a son in the explosion.

"I been lookin' at the buffalo," Kelly said.

"What about 'em?"

"Wonderin' why they didn't react to the explosion."

Ellis squinted out at the herd that was moving a little more restlessly, but showed no indications of being startled by the explosion of the powder car. "You'd think they'd rustle a bit," Ellis said thoughtfully.

"Think somebody's out there cooling them down?"

"Like who?"

"Like Goose Face."

Ellis wondered. No one could control buffalo, but he had heard that some of the plains Indians could work among them—"talking buffalo," as the story went.

"I have a favor to ask of you, lad," Kelly began.

"Sorry, Kelly." Ellis shook his head. "I been lookin' for Lefty too long a time."

"I haven't asked you yet."

"Then don't. I'm sorry you got yourself a peck of trouble—losing your scout, this explosion, maybe Goose Face, too—but you don't know how long I been trailin' this fellow."

"Would you want me to send off a greenhorn that would get stomped to death by the buffalo even if he managed to escape a Cheyenne arrow?

"If he's foolish enough to go, it's his lookout," Ellis said brusquely. "I thought you was gunned-up ready to take a look." He nodded at the old Colt Kelly still wore.

"I can't leave now," Kelly said worriedly. "I've got to see to everything here."

"Then you got yourself one more problem, Kelly." And Ellis started to walk away.

"Where you going?" Kelly called after him.

"Lookin' for Lefty Hayes."

The tall Texan worked his way through the tents and headed for Watson's. The pole had been jacked up and the canvas was fluttering in the hot southwestern wind.

* * *

Watson's tent was nearly full now. The rough plank bar was crowded and the bartenders were hard-pressed to keep up with the orders. The women were still chattering in the corner, but a few had moved to the bar among the men and were drinking the whisky from the earthen crocks.

Simpson and Garrity still flanked the opening to the tent when Ellis came up to it. Simpson stood up and hooked his thumbs lightly over his gunbelt. "Stay right where you are, big boy. You ain't allowed."

Ellis stopped in his tracks. "You figurin' on stoppin' me?"

"I'm going to try," Simpson said loudly. "If you get past me, Garrity will take over, and there's nine more inside just like us. Now you figure it out."

Ellis's hand moved to his thigh and came up full of Colt, hammer back and rock-steady. Simpson had not even unhooked his thumbs. He stared at Ellis in amazement and raised his hands. Without being told to, Garrity raised his hands too. "I ain't interested in the odds," Ellis said coolly. "Just information. Is a man named Lefty Hayes inside?"

"Lefty?" Simpson glanced at Garrity. "Whatcha want with Lefty?"

45

"Answer the question!" Ellis rapped out.

"Lefty ain't here, mister," Garrity said. "He rode on west last week to Green River, but he's expected back tonight."

"Is he tellin' me the truth?" Ellis demanded of Simpson.

"That's the truth. You got a hassle with Lefty?"

"I have."

"You going to have a shoot-out?"

"If he'll stand up and face me, we will." Ellis's voice was hard.

"Lefty'll do that, mister. Yes sir, if you'll just gimme your name, I'll tell Lefty you was lookin' for him."

"The name don't matter," Ellis said, putting his Colt away. "Just say Sky Rock. He'll know."

"Sky Rock. I'll sure tell him," Simpson said interestedly, and the moment that Nathan Ellis turned away, the two men hurried inside the tent and searched out Jeremy Watson.

* * *

Liza Reeves strode up to Kelly. With a toss of her head she dismissed his thanks for her help during the past terrible moments.

"When you figure you'll be ridin' out to look for Jake?"

Kelly pointed to the sweating men laboring to repair the track. "I can't leave now, miss."

"Then I'll go," Liza said with decision. "I don't figure it's likely that Jake ran into any trouble, mind you. It's just that I ain't seen him in a year and a half and I'm outa patience waitin'."

46

"I wouldn't, if I was in your place, miss," Kelly said. "Of course, I haven't had too much experience with Indians. But what little I've had's taught me to be mighty wary."

"You don't need to fear none for me, mister. I don't guess Jake did much talkin' 'bout me, or you'd know I was raised with a doll made outa Cheyenne hair and cut my teeth on a Sioux arrowhead." Her eyes glowed. "I got me some Sioux when they raided our place and orphaned me and Jake. Ol' Jake got a lot of 'em too. We was buryin' Sioux for two weeks afterward." Then she added, "Jake was fourteen and me nine."

"Where was that?"

"Up in the headwaters of the Little Missouri."

"And you live up there alone?"

"I got me a coupla crippled-up Sioux that live with me. We sorta adopted each other when our folks was killed. Jake lit out when he was a youngun, wanted to go fight in the war for the Yankees. Then when he come back, he couldn't be satisfied with trappin' and huntin' any more. And it didn't look like he was gonna get him a woman that'd come live up there with him, so he came back down to Omaha and that's where he hooked up with you, I reckon." Her eyes wandered to the buffalo. "So I guess I'll just get my horse and spread out west yonder till I find him." She nodded. "I'm hungry for a talk with ol' Jake."

Kelly thought he saw concern in her eyes. "I had intended asking the general to send out a squad of troopers," he lied.

Liza snorted. "And what would they see? They'd raise enough dust out yonder to warn the gophers they was comin'."

"Well, I can't stop you, Miss Reeves. And I can't give you any information about where your brother might be at this time. The survey engineers and graders returned early this mornin' and said they saw a fire about thirty miles west of the trailhead. Thought it might be Jake."

"At night?" Liza asked quickly.

"Yes, I guess so."

Her eyes flashed. "Then it wasn't Jake," she said tonelessly. "He'd know better than to set a fire on the plains. Any good scout would know that. Give his position and presence away. I better get out and start huntin'." She was turning to leave just as Nathan Ellis strode up.

"My man won't be around until tonight, Kelly," he said, watching Liza. "So I guess I'll just take a little look out there beyond them buffalo a ways. If Goose Face is around here, I'd like to have a try at him. Him and his party killed two good friends of mine."

"I'll ride with you," Liza said.

"Where can I get a good pony, Kelly?" Ellis ignored her. "I don't like to ride scout unless I got an animal that can run for me."

"Take mine, lad. The Jehu in my tent will give you what you need," Kelly said eagerly. "And consider yourself on the payroll of the Union Pacific Railroad, as of this minute."

"You heard what I said," Liza Reeves insisted. "I said I was ridin' with you."

Ellis turned his back on her and drawled to Kelly, "I don't want no pay. I ain't got much to do until Lefty shows up tonight, anyhow, and if I can help get Goose Face, why, I'd consider that a good turn all around."

48

Kelly's eyes began to twinkle as he saw how Liza Reeves flushed with anger.

"You got any objections to my riding' with you?" she demanded.

"Why no, ma'am," Ellis said elaborately. "If you got a good animal under you and want to keep me company, why I'd welcome it."

"I got the best critter outa the whole Dakotas."

"I guess you have got a good walk-in' horse." Ellis grinned. "Trottin' down from the Missouri country like you did."

"*Walkin'* horse!" Liza Reeves exploded. "My critter will run dog-legged anything you could straddle!"

"Now I'd like to see somethin' that swift, wouldn't you, Mr. Kelly?"

Kelly indicated that he wanted none of it, and turned his attention to the laboring Johnny-Jacks and bellowed a command.

"You figure to let me see this spirited horse before we ride outa camp?"

Liza Reeves stamped off in the direction of Kelly's tent. Ellis followed with a wink at the grinning Irishman.

Kelly's Jehu had saddled a big roan stallion for Ellis and now the tall Texan followed a very angry Liza Reeves.

"There he is," Liza said, pointing to a sturdy gray.

Ellis frowned, and then shrugged. "Well, ma'am, it's a horse."

Liza Reeves clenched her teeth and strode to her horse and slapped its flank. Without glancing at Ellis, she threw the brightly colored saddle blanket across the gray's back, swang the heavy saddle up and reached under the animal's belly for the cinch straps.

"You better let me pull that up for you, miss," Ellis said agreeably.

"I can do it," she grunted.

Ellis elbowed his way closer to the horse and took the cinch strap from her. He pulled and forked it in. "There you are."

He turned to the stallion and swung lightly into the saddle. "Let's go," he said, and turned his mount west through the tents.

Liza Reeves swung into her saddle and lightly put her spurs to the gray. The gray bucked straight up, twisted, and threw her into the mud. Liza looked at her horse as if the beast had suddenly gone mad. She remounted, and as soon as her weight settled on the gray's back, it bucked with all four legs and threw her again.

She rose, wary now, and tried to coax the gray closer so that she could reach the reins. Then she saw the sand sticker on the underside of the blanket.

"That no-good, low-down, crawlin' Texan!" Liza Reeves said hoarsely. "I'll get him—" And she tried, with the help of the grinning Jehu, to calm her snorting gray.

* * *

By now Goose Face had maneuvered to the north of the railhead with his party and, like the good warrior he was, had cut back to the south alone to check the position of the buffalo herd and the progress of the railhead, and to learn the reason for the explosion earlier.

He saw the devastation caused by the powder car, and he saw the quick work being done to repair it. Then

50

something else caught his eye. A lone rider had struck to the west, riding hard and fast across the flat grass country, his big roan kicking up the dust and leaving a trail high and heavy in the noonday sun.

His second group of braves would take care of that rider, Goose Face thought confidently, and swung his pony back toward his main group. Nothing had changed. The long beards would die in great numbers on their Sad-a-day feast, and he, Soft-and-Running-Deer, would repay in part for the slaughter of his people on the edges of Sandy Creek.

Chapter Three

ONCE WELL AWAY from the railhead, Ellis swung south of the great herd of buffalo and loped steadily down in the direction of the ridge country of the South Platte. He rode with his head bowed before the high sun, legs loose and out of the stirrups. Now and then he swung a leg over the saddle-horn as a rider does who has covered a great distance, or is in no hurry to make time across the summer-hot plains.

All the while he scanned the horizon for signs of life—Cheyenne life—turning occasionally to cover his trail, eyes steady for the dust cloud that would indicate another rider.

He topped a rise and dropped into a draw, got off his pony and sat cross-legged in its shadow. He rolled a cigarette and stared moodily before him, his short, breech-loading carbine across his lap.

He finished the cigarette, stood up and remounted. He pulled the roan back up the dry wash bed and moved on up to a swell of sand hills and stared back over his trail from the railhead. He watched the rim of the horizon for ten minutes, scanning a full circle, then abruptly whipped the stallion around with a jerk and pounded back into the draw and toward the buffalo herd, but well west of it now.

The roan's hoofs kicked up dust in a high, billowing cloud, but Ellis didn't care, for he knew that there was nothing behind him.

* * *

As a boy Ellis had drifted with the buffalo hunters up from the Texas Panhandle, and he knew the simple greed of the Cheyenne when in close proximity to buffalo. Indeed, the desire for a bloody cut of under-belly from a young buffalo calf, or a chunk from the small hump behind the beast's neck, was known to any man who had ever cut the spine of a buffalo and butchered him on the spot. Ellis was counting on the nearness of the herd to draw the followers of Goose Face out into the open, if they were near. If there were a hundred and twenty of them, Ellis reasoned, there would be some mighty hungry Indians staring down at the herd. And Goose Face would have to be a mighty tough Cheyenne with much strong medicine to keep him from trying for the bloody guts of an eighteen-hundred-pound bull animal. For when the buffalo was near and in great quantities, the plains Indians had food, clothing and shelter. They did not plant corn as did the tribes to the east that lived near the Missouri. Many of the western nomadic tribes believed the greatest medicine was the skin of a white buffalo. With this powerful culture working on his side, Ellis was sure that, one way or another, the Cheyenne following Goose Face would ride against the herd, or work downwind of it, and try for a straggler with arrow or rifle.

Nathan Ellis had loved this big country since the first day he had stood in stupefaction and awe before the eight-hundred-foot height of Scotts bluff hanging over the Platte. Here was a country a boy could love, in which he could grow into a man feeling a part of it, and watch his children grow into men. Often Nathan Ellis found himself in sympathy with the red men who had had this great world all to themselves, as a garden of paradise to range over and live in. No wonder they fell back on the bitterest savagery to resist having it wrested from them.

Ellis had ridden in a wide semi-circle, appreciative of Kelly's strong, tireless roan, when he stopped, suddenly, with a sharp tug at the hand lines.

He stood in the middle of a flat bed of grass that brushed the belly of the stallion, about three thousand yards away from the nearest sand spur. "Steady, hoss," he said softly, patting the animal on the neck. "Somethin's stirrin' round here."

The roan settled, though Ellis felt the animal quiver along the spine. He strained his ears to pick up some sound, but could hear nothing.

He kneed the animal in the ribs gently and clucked his tongue, head and eyes moving constantly. The grass rippled around the roan's shanks, and then Ellis slipped out of the saddle and moved expertly and quickly in the direction of a sandy hillock. At five hundred yards from the rise, he dropped to his knees and went forward on all fours, slinking the carbine alongside of him. All but hidden in the tall, swaying grass, he inched to the top of the spur.

Parting the grass with the barrel of his carbine, Ellis lay flat on his belly and grinned down at the scene below him. Three Cheyenne were spread downwind of a huge buffalo bull and were now making signs as to how they should attack. One of them had a muzzle loader with a barrel nearly four feet long and was hurriedly dumping powder into the pan. The other Indians watched the armed brave pull the hammer back gently. Ellis could see them holding their breaths when the cocking broke the silence.

The old bull raised his head and turned to stare at them, not actually seeing them but curious about the click. Then he dropped his head and continued nuzzling the long grass.

54

The other two braves moved quickly, strung arrows in curved bone bows and set themselves. At a signal that Ellis did not see, the armed brave stood up, took steady and careful aim and fired.

The bull raised his head unhurriedly and stared at the noise and at the standing man.

One of the braves rose and shot an arrow. The bull decided on the Indian with the gun and charged.

Quickly the third brave stood up and threw an arrow. He caught the bull in the right fore-flank, but the beast continued to come as if unharmed. Now Ellis saw the gaping wound in the buffalo's neck. The brave with the gun had tried for a brain shot behind the ear and had missed.

The first bowman ran in close, ten feet away from the charging beast, and fired an arrow at an angle designed to reach the heart.

He must have missed because the buffalo caught the brave with the gun in the belly with his horns and ripped him open. The Indian spun away, holding his spilling guts, and staggered several feet before he stopped, reeled and dropped in the grass.

The bull, head down, charged for the finish, but the bowmen had restrung. They moved in broadside and fired their shafts, again behind the flank and aiming for the heart.

The bull jerked sideways, stumbled cross-legged and nearly fell. Then, spread-legged, he charged again.

Ellis watched it all—the grim struggle of the bull and the plains Indians who had to kill him in order to live. He had seen it enacted a hundred times before. He found himself breathing hard, rooting for both sides at once— for the magnificent old bull, stupid with strength, and for the lithe, swift braves.

A second brave went down from the buffalo's charging horns, but the bull was weak and nearly gone. The third brave moved around to the other side of the animal to drive home a lance, and Ellis saw at once that it was a fatal mistake.

The brave steadied himself and raised the lance. The bull swung his head in a semi-circle, sweeping up, not to attack so much as to see where his adversary was. His horns caught the brave in the thigh, laying him open up to the hip. Even from the rise, Ellis could see the white of the exposed thigh bone.

The brave dropped the lance and fell back. Then, with tottering strength, the bull turned awkwardly and moved to gore the wounded Indian. He missed with his head and staggered forward. As he staggered, he pushed out a foreleg for balance. The hoof and six inches of the bull's shank disappeared into the chest cavity of the fallen brave. The brave screamed, pinned to the ground by the buffalo's hoof, and then he relaxed in death.

The buffalo spread his legs trying to keep his balance, and Ellis could see the knuckle joints quiver as the strength ebbed out of the huge black beast.

The bull sagged to his fore-joints, then rolled over on top of two of his attackers.

The whole encounter had lasted not more than three minutes.

Ellis lay perfectly still, to see if the gunshot would bring anyone, before returning to his pony. The animal had been well trained. It had not moved out of its tracks.

Riding over the crest of the sand spur, Ellis dropped down onto the plains and gentled his roan when the animal smelled the blood. Dismounting, Ellis examined each dead brave closely and confirmed what he had suspected.

They were Cheyenne, all right, but their leggings and moccasins were very old and ragged. It had been a long time since these braves had returned to their lodges where their squaws would have new ones waiting for them.

Ellis looked around carefully for the ponies of the dead braves, but he saw nothing. That could only mean one thing: other braves would be returning for them. The attempted kill of the old bull, the biggest buffalo Ellis had ever seen, must have been planned, with riders dropping off their horses some distance away and coming up, downwind of the beast, on foot.

There was a moan, a low wail and Ellis spun around, his Colt ready. One of the braves was still alive. Ellis moved among them and saw that it was the first of the three, still holding his stomach. Ellis pulled his knife to cut the brave's throat as an act of mercy. Then he stopped short.

When the others came after these three, it would be plain that one of them had been slit, and not by the old bull. If Ellis had any hope of trailing the new arrivals back to Goose Face's camp, he would have to let this brave writhe in pain and die in agony out here on the plains.

In the distance he heard the cry of a wolf that had picked up the blood scent miles away. Ellis glanced around once more, and then swung into the saddle and loped slowly back up the sand spur, turning to see the plains grass sweep back over his roan's tracks and hiding them forever. Soothing his mount with soft words and caresses on the neck, Ellis got the big stallion to lie flat in the grass deep on the farther side of the rise, and stretched out, belly-down, himself.

His body stiffened against the piercing shricks of the brave dying on the other side of the spur. Then he heard

57

a low growl, and suddenly the blood-curdling howl of a wolf. He knew a plains jackal had committed the final coup on the disemboweled brave.

* * *

It was not long before the second party of braves arrived. Ellis heard them when they were still some distance away, on the opposite side of the spur. He could imagine them urging their ponies ahead to the scene and he listened for their voices to rise when they discovered the deaths.

He understood a great deal of what they said to each other, and they were as impressed with the size of the bull and with the obvious struggle of their slain comrades as they were with the fact that nothing lived. Their feelings for the slain Indians were genuine but short-lived. Soon Ellis heard them begin the skinning and quartering of the huge buffalo.

He judged it to be close to one in the afternoon when he heard them begin to move off. He waited, tense, and then, with a reassuring pat to the stallion, he snaked his way to the ridge of the spur. A band of eight, the spare ponies of the dead braves slung heavy with sides of dripping beef, moved off to the northeast. The guts, bones and hoofs were all that remained of the bull buffalo. The three slain braves were left to the wolves, vultures and maggots. They had not been buried. Only the renegade brave, who had broken away from all tribal culture, would leave another brave unprotected in death, especially in such an honorable death.

Wary of the wolves that were now growing in number and tearing at the remains of the buffalo and the dead men, Ellis moved back to his roan and swung into the saddle. He topped the spur and slowly, with great patience, began trailing after the Cheyenne party.

Chapter Four

JAKE REEVES had once been captured by the Blackfeet, along with an old trapper who put him wise to the contradictions of the Indian mind. "One minute," the trapper said, "you'll find an Injun to be as wise as Solomon and the next minute caperin' 'round with a piece of lookin' glass like a ninny bitter. But there ain't nothin' a redskin likes to do more than show off. He loves to strut and dance and sing and make medicine, but when he's huntin' or out on a war party, he's dead serious. Best goddam fightin' man in the world, considerin' he usually ain't got nothin' but a hoss and a bow 'n' arrow, standin' up to his fight naked as a jay bird. And when he's fightin' he's already thinkin' how he's gonna dance and make medicine when he gets back to his lodge.

"And part of that palaver he's plannin' is torturing his captured enemy. He figures to kill you anyway, so he might as well have a little fun, and show off in the bargain. Now, if you stand up to it like a man, and take the torturin', it just makes him that much bigger in the eyes of the squaw and the other braves that he was able to capture a man as brave as you. On the other hand, if you give up and start whinin' and beggin', you're makin' a ridicule outa him, so he'll likely kill you for embarrasssin' him, 'cause capturin' a whinin' beggar ain't no coup. Now, boy, if they really got you, you ain't likely to get away, so the only chance you got is to work on his pride and the yes-and-no, because it is and it ain't part of the savage's make-up.

"When he comes to torture you, stand up to him. Don't be sassy 'cause he'll just ram a Green River in you and gut you. No, boy, you gotta play off the contradictions, the

59

pride and man part of him against the little kid part of him. Now, how you do that is dependin' a whole hell of a lot on what particular Injun's got you. If you're lucky to be caught by a chief, or a medicine man, you stand a better chance 'cause the whole shebang is watchin' him and he's gotta put on a good show. That's important, boy, puttin' on a good show.

"Killin' ain't no more than blowin' your nose to an Injun, so just killin' a captured enemy don't mean much. You have to make him look good. Now, you might be able to do it this way, boy. Listen good, 'cause leastways you might have a chance.

"When he starts to give you a rassle, torturin' you one way or another, take it without battin' an eyelash. And then when he's struttin' before the women and the kids and the other braves, you have to indicate that it was luck that let him get you. See what I mean, boy? You gotta get across the idea that you'd like to just set the record straight—mind you, not challenge him, or call him a liar, 'cause that'd be interpreted as beggin'. You just gotta ease it into his mind that the others watchin' don't believe his tale about how he got you. It ain't the others you gotta convince, it's him. Put it in his mind that they don't believe his story and, boy, you gotta chance to meet him with tommy-hawks, or bow 'n' arrow, or over the steel of a Green River blade. That's the only chance you got, boy, and if you whip him, ain't a nation of Injuns livin' that'd knife you in the back. I tell you, boy, it's the only chance you got."

The boy Reeves, sixteen and strong as a bull, had nimbly maneuvered a giant Blackfoot brave that day into fighting a duel to the death with naked knives before the hoots and hussahs of the Blackfoot's village. Jake Reeves still wore the jagged pink scar along his upper belly where the brave's knife had narrowly missed a death lunge, and the boy fighter had successfully countered with his own knife, driving it up to the hilt into the Indian's stomach.

The old trapper had been burned to death at the stake, a victim of his own plan when his captor had simply dismissed the old man's suggestions that he was a coward, with a tomahawk blow between the eyes.

In later years, as he grew older and wiser in experience in the ways of the Indian mind, Jake Reeves had fought four such challenges and walked away from them. He became a friend to many tribes because of his reputation with a Green River blade and because of his honesty. He had carved out a special place for himself and for his sister in the heart of the Missouri country. The two of them became known as Big and Little Sand Sticker, because to hold one tightly was impossible without drawing blood.

But Goose Face was a bitter and wise brave. He had learned the white man's lesson of war simply and effectively. Take any advantage, offer no quarter and don't succumb to the cleverness of the white man's mind. When you have him, kill him. Don't talk, don't hesitate, just kill him. Jake Reeves's attempts to force Goose Face into personal combat before the other renegades had not worked. The young rebel savage had simply whacked Reeves on the head with his rifle and ordered him spread and pegged to the ground in the bottom of the draw.

The scout had been pinned to the ground since the night before. The sun had burned down on him since dawn and his tongue had swollen from thirst. He had listened to Goose Face's plan to stampede the buffalo into the railhead, and attack from the east at the same time, and he knew that since it was Saturday the Johnny-Jacks would be dead drunk, to the man, crowding Watson's grog tents.

When Goose Face had split up the party, leaving twenty braves behind to stampede the herd, Reeves had hoped for one thing: that the remaining braves would not be able to resist taking one buffalo while they waited. It was the last thing Jake Reeves remembered before he fainted beneath the sun. One of the sentinels had spotted a huge bull—from the talk, the biggest ever seen—wandering away from the herd. Reeves had listened to them argue. Many were afraid of Goose Face and contended that they should remain in the draw until it was time to attack the railhead. Others insisted that they had a right to eat. Eventually a plan was decided on to take the single, huge buffalo. Lots were drawn to see who would go. Half of the stampede party rode out of the draw; it was then that Jake Reeves slid into unconsciousness.

He was still unconscious when the party returned talking of the fight that must have taken place between the giant bull and the three braves. It was from such stories that legends began and grew in the lodges of the plains people.

* * *

When Nathan Ellis saw the party of Cheyenne approach a draw beyond a small rise, he recognized the position. He stopped his roan and flanked out away from the rise, wary of being spotted by sentinels he knew would be watching. He dropped back to the east, rounded a swell and pulled the stallion down still. There before him, five miles away, were the buffalo, and beyond, shimmering like a mirage in the afternoon heat, was the railhead camp.

Moving back away from the draw and well west of the buffalo, Ellis dismounted and hobbled the roan. He removed his carbine and rawhide lariat and slung his canteen over his shoulder. Going fast and low in the belt-high grass, he angled off well west of the draw.

* * *

When Liza Reeves finally caught her snorting gray, she pulled the sand sticker from beneath the blanket and swung into the saddle, her face contorted with rage. She slapped the pony hard on the rump, cleared tent guys and stays in leaps that startled dogs and scattered chickens, and struck straight west.

She rode low in the saddle, head forward, braced against the stirrups and the motion of the gray. She moved to the north of the buffalo, cutting right across the railhead where the Johnny-Jacks were laying rail faster than it had ever been put down before in the entire world.

She knew Nathan Ellis had gone south of the herd and, ordinarily, she would have lifted the high dust in that direction herself, but her anger was working hand-in-hand with her obstinance. To hell with him, she thought, that smart rebel critter! I'll just ride north and cut back around the head of the buffalo, and have a look-see into that rise beyond.

Knowing the habits of her brother, knowing nearly as much about the trail as he did and completely dismissing the idea that anything could have happened to him, she tipped the edge of the herd and cut back toward the rise. As she approached, she noted that the buffalo, who were grazing all the while but moving nevertheless, had made a circuit away from the rise.

She pulled the gray down and stopped, stood in the saddle and smelled the air. She caught the faint tang of brush-wood smoke, and then searched for a visible sign.

She laughed suddenly. "Of course," she said to herself. "Jake wouldn't make a fire anybody could see."

She nudged the gray broomtail forward toward the rise, her nose catching stronger suggestions of smoke as she moved.

Liza was not so enthusiastic to see her brother as to throw caution to the winds. She was aware that the fire could just as easily have been made by Indians, but she did not believe they would cut out a buffalo from the herd and feast on him with the railhead moving so fast, nearer all the time. More likely, she reasoned, there wasn't a redskin in a thirty-mile reach of here. A big party with much medicine would hesitate before going after the buffalo so close to the railhead, and a small party simply wouldn't dare.

She slapped her knees against the gray's ribs and touched him with her wang reins. The animal spurted forward toward the rise.

* * *

Ellis snaked belly-down through the tall grass. Above him an old Cheyenne warrior, who had lost his hair many years before in some forgotten brush with another nation, sat cross-legged atop a round of grass-covered clay, an outcropping of the rise above the draw.

The brave's attention was pulled back into the draw itself and his sweeping search of the plains east to the buffalo and the railhead became less and less frequent. When Ellis smelled the brush smoke, he grinned to himself. The Cheyenne were taking their time with the buffalo and not eating it raw, but were roasting it instead.

The Cheyenne sentinel waved his arms and yelled something to the other brave beyond the round out of

Ellis's view. He was getting angry, Ellis thought, and hungry. Someone answered him, but the old brave did not reply. He swept his eyes around the plains and then turned his body around to address himself more fully to the activity in the draw.

Ellis drew his Bowie and clamped it between his teeth. He inched forward, bringing the lariat up and slipping the eye down to make a tight, eighteen-inch loop. He judged the Cheyenne to be about twenty feet away from him, pulled off that many coils, looped them in his left and hand waited.

The Cheyenne did not move. Ellis watched the high grass atop the round and when it began to waver a bit, he tightened up. The grass bent in a sudden hot gust of wind. Ellis jerked up and flew the lariat against the wind, up and out. It faltered and appeared to drop short. He was ready with the Bowie when the loop dropped neatly over the brave's head. He jerked hard and what little out- cry the Indian made was carried away by the gust and not heard in the draw.

With quick strides, Ellis was beside the brave, who struggled in the grass against the rawhide lariat. Without hesitation, Ellis rammed the Bowie into the Indian's back. The knife struck bone and then slipped past and into the heart. The old warrior died without a sound.

Ellis pushed the grass aside to stare down into the draw. All of the remaining braves were hacking away at the dripping sides of beef, gesturing and talking rapidly. Further to one side Ellis spotted the spread-eagled form of Jake Reeves.

He moved back and to the higher point on the round, searching for the second sentinel he was sure would be placed farther to the east. He stopped some fifty yards farther up the rim of the draw, and waited.

He did not wait long. A garish face, old and seamed, peered up out of the grass and stared down into the draw at the other braves.

Ellis grinned.

Snaking his way back to the dead Cheyenne, the Texan removed a double curved Nez Percé bone bow the old warrior had probably received in a trade many years before, and slipped a feathered shaft from the fur quiver. Stringing the arrow, he tested the power of the bow and decided it would kill at fifty yards. Then he slipped away toward the farther end of the round.

The second sentinel did not show himself for nearly five minutes. All that time Ellis was inching forward. He was nearly forty yards away, still hidden by the plains grass, when the Indian showed himself. Ellis lifted up to one knee, pulled down on the powerful bow and sighted briefly on the Indian's chest.

The arrow sang eerily in the silence. A second later Ellis heard the dull *thunk* of the shaft finding its mark.

The moment he had shot the arrow, Ellis grabbed his carbine and moved toward the top of the round overlooking the draw. He did not expect the second Indian to die without a sound as conveniently as the first had, and he wanted to be in a commanding position above the feasting party below.

His luck held. The second Cheyenne made less noise than the sing of the arrow, and Ellis found himself overlooking the draw, where more than a dozen unsuspecting braves gorged themselves on buffalo meat.

Ellis's face tightened at the sight of Jake Reeves.

66

He threw down on the party and fired at a Cheyenne. The man dropped in his tracks, a good part of his head torn off. The others looked upward in stunned silence.

Ellis raised the carbine again. "Let the long beard go," he said in his best Cheyenne. "Drop your weapons."

The Indians did not move. Ellis fired again. A second warrior dropped like a stone. The braves allowed their weapons to fall to the ground.

Two of them went to Jake Reeves and began to release him. The absence of Goose Face intensified the already growing suspicion in Ellis's mind that this was an advance party sent here—or left in the draw—for some savage reason of the renegade leader.

Ellis indicated that he wanted the scout put on a pony and brought up to the ridge of the rise. Jabbering among themselves, and looking up at the round where the sentinels should have been, the party slopped water into Jake's face and made efforts to bring him to. A horse was brought from the end of the draw and the scout was lifted, ungently, onto the animal's back. As one of the braves stepped forward to lead the broomtail up to Ellis, a bloodcurdling scream ripped the hot afternoon quiet.

Ellis spun around. On the round where he had slain the second sentinel, a brave held Liza Reeves by the hair with one hand and brandished a blade across her throat with the other.

Even from this distance Ellis could make out the disfigured face of the Cheyenne and knew that it was Goose Face.

Chapter Five

IN BROKEN ENGLISH that was thick with the "K" sounds of the Cheyenne tongue, Goose Face screamed his threats across the rise. "She die! She die! You stop! She die!" Goose Face cried. Then, turning to the braves in the draw who stood transfixed at the quickness of events, the renegade leader ordered them up to Ellis. The tall Texan gripped the carbine tightly, knowing that if he fired or resisted, Liza Reeves would die instantly. She may die anyway, Ellis thought, but at the moment he had no choice.

"Shoot 'em! Shoot 'em! Liza Reeves shouted across to him "He'll kill me anyways!" Goose Face jerked her backward by the hair and slapped her hard across the face.

Ellis made his decision. He jerked up his carbine to take aim on the Cheyenne leader when half a dozen pairs of hands pulled at him from below. Ellis fought back violently, kicking, biting, wrenching, but it was futile. The braves overpowered him with brute strength. There was a violent pain in the back of his head and Ellis felt himself sinking willingly into the arms of the braves, and then came a blackness that was not penetrated even by the white-hot Nebraska sun.

* * *

When Goose Face had cut back to view the railhead and explore the reason for the explosion, he had lingered long enough to see a second rider in buckskin cutting to the north.

Goose Face had not hesitated. He had jerked his pony and pounded even further to the north, cut back beyond the buffalo, and drew up well west of the draw where

68

he had left his stampede party. From deep in the high plains grass he had watched Ellis make his approach to the round and slay two of his braves. He was on his way to cut the tall Texan down from behind, when he sighted the woman. His crafty mind saw a ripe opportunity, and he circled the draw and came up behind Liza Reeves. His medicine was working well for him. The rider was a woman. Goose Face knew there was nothing the whites prized more than their squaws.

He squatted now in the hot sun before the three pegged and spread figures, wondering what advantage he could make out of their capture.

His horribly mutilated face had been painted dead white and two slashes of vermilion angled from his ears down to the gash of his mouth. His lower lip had been cut away and his bottom teeth were long and looked like fangs where the gums had dried and shrunk nearly to the roots.

He stood up. "Nothing has change," he said to one of his braves. "And these whites will help us. Slay them and tie them to horses when you stampede the buffalo. They will run before the herd."

"What advantage is that to us?" a buck asked.

Goose Face moved his head violently with annoyance. "When the long beards see the buffalo, they will send out riders and long knives to fire into the herd and turn them away from the trail of the smoking horse. If they see that whites are running before the herd, they will not shoot with such ease for fear of hitting them. They will not turn the buffalo. Then we attack in their confusion."

He swung up onto his pony. "Slay them when the sun is there." He pointed into the sky. "And lash them well to their horses."

Goose Face whipped his pony out of the draw and pounded west and north to catch up with his main party.

Other sentinels were posted on the round and the remaining bucks continued to eat. They were more subdued now and never took their eyes from the three figures spread on the ground.

* * *

"Pssst!" Liza Reeves made a sound against her teeth, closing her eyes against the sun and turning her head a fraction of an inch at a time toward her right.

Ellis, five feet away from her, grunted softly. His head ached and he wanted desperately to touch it. He had awakened from a short nightmare in which a squaw was lifting his hair with a red-hot knife and gouging out his eyes with a heated tong.

"Can you see if they're still eatin'?" she asked so quietly that Ellis was not sure she had spoken. He flopped his head to one side and stared at her. She mouthed the words with her lips. He understood then and, groaning as if in pain, twisted his body as much as possible to glance over at the braves sitting beside their ponies. It was close to two o'clock and the sun was still high, though shadows were beginning to favor the eastern side of the broomtails.

"Yes," he said in a whisper.

"How many close to me?"

"Three. About thirty feet away." He kept his head turned the other way so that the bucks would think he was mumbling in unconscious pain.

"When they stop eatin', they might go to sleep," she said hopefully. "I got my left hand loose—"

She stopped abruptly as she heard the soft footsteps of an approaching brave. She lay still.

The Indian squatted beside her and stared into her face. He did not touch her at first. He cocked his head from side to side examining her figure stretched in the dust. Slowly the brave extended his hand and stroked her cheek. He spoke to someone behind him and pulled her head to one side roughly and examined the thick mat of her hair.

The brave stood up and moved back to his pony and squatted in its shadow. He spoke to several others, softly, casually.

"One of 'em likes you," Ellis said in a mumble of pain.

"Which one?"

"The big one. I think he's after your hair."

The brave got up from among his companions and moved back again toward Liza Reeves. He squatted beside her once more.

Liza Reeves opened her eyes and stared into his face. She smiled. It was not easy to keep her eyes open against the sun, but she stared at the brave, smiling, until his face wavered and danced, finally disappearing altogether in the tears that run from her eyes. But before she had been blinded by the sun, she had seen that the brave carried a Green River knife, a belt hatchet and a heavy Colt. It was not hers. She guessed it to be one taken from Ellis or from Jake.

She opened her eyes and looked up at the brave. She moaned and began moving her lips. Her eyes full on the Indian, she made sounds in her throat and writhed in the dust in unmistakable signs of passion that went beyond any language barrier.

The brave spoke to her. He began to grin and turned to speak to his companions, who laughed and got up to come and watch the fun.

The brave pulled the buckskin belt from around Liza Reeves's waist and jerked at her leather blouse. He slit the top of her trousers with his knife and tore the leather away from her body.

The braves laughed and commented on the whiteness of Liza's body and urged the brave on.

She had not stopped twisting and writhing her hips in the dust and moaning with passion. She held her eyes tight against the sun and pulled her hand through the leather thongs that held it, to a point where it could be pulled out easily.

The brave dropped on top of her to the loud cheers and laughter of the other braves.

Liza's hand pulled free from the thong pegged in the ground and slipped to the brave's belt. She had the Colt out and shoved it against the Indian's belly. The brave had not let his full weight down upon her when she fired, the force of the bullet throwing him away from her.

Liza shot the three braves standing beside her before they realized what had happened. The others were well up the draw, which gave her just enough time to grab the blade from the first brave and slash at her bound right hand. She did not have time to cut her feet free. She snatched up the Colt again and fired twice, killing two braves bearing down on her with knives.

Fifty feet away, a brave saw what was happening and dropped to his knee. He strung an arrow and pulled down on her. She ducked behind one of the dead bodies and grabbed the knife. The arrow sank into the dead man, going clear through him and burying its head an inch in Liza's shoulder. The Indian strung a second arrow and stood up to advance more closely. Liza pushed the dead brave to one side and let go with the knife. The heavy Green River blade whistled through the air and caught the buck in the throat. He sank back, jerking at the knife, and began to cough.

Liza grabbed the belt hatchet and chopped her leg thongs away from the pegs. Free now, she ran toward the horses and found what she was looking for—Ellis's carbine that lay in the dust where one of the Indians had dropped it.

The remaining members of the stampede party had moved to the top of the draw and were now slinging arrows at her. Liza tried to keep behind the pony, but the animal was frightened and jumped away. An arrow caught it in the rump and it screamed with pain.

Liza leveled the carbine at the beast's head and fired. The animal staggered and dropped. Liza forted up behind it and began firing coolly and methodically at the Indians on top of the draw.

"Get me free, God damn it!" Ellis roared.

"I will! I will!" Liza shouted, and went on shooting.

Ellis's yell drew attention away from Liza, and one of the braves steadied an arrow at Jake. The arrow sang in the air and buried itself in the scout's head. Liza turned in time to see her brother die, without a sound.

Enraged, she stood up and, still firing at the group on top of the draw, ran to Ellis's side. Arrows sailed around her, and one buried itself in the fleshy part of her thigh, but she continued, slashing at the thongs that bound Ellis's right hand. Freeing the hand, she dropped the knife to let him finish cutting himself loose and began to fire more carefully.

The braves were a little more cautious now that Liza had killed the one who had stood up briefly to release his shaft. She kept moving at a half-run back and forth across the bottom of the draw, scanning the top of the rise and firing only when one of the braves dared to attempt to loose a shaft.

Ellis was free now and had gathered in the discarded Colt where Liza had dropped it. He reloaded and shouted for her to head toward the west end of the draw where most of the horses were tethered.

They half ran, half staggered toward the horses, Ellis hardly able to see through the glare of the naked burning sun.

The braves followed them along the top of the rise and continued to sling arrows on them indiscriminately. Three broomtails were hit. The animals screamed and bucked against their halters and kicked out in pain.

Ellis threw the Colt to Liza and grabbed the carbine in order to reload. Still firing at the braves who were trying to circle around them, Liza slashed at the rawhide that held the horses. She swung up on the back of the nearest and shouted at Ellis. "Let's go!"

The tall Texan leaped on the back of a pony and then they kicked their mounts hard in the flanks and sent them racing down the draw over the dead braves. The remaining horses, free of their restraint, galloped alongside of them.

The two riders struck straight to the west at a dead gallop. Behind them, the Cheyenne were scurrying after their ponies, and three were already riding out after them.

They had a lead of about half a mile on the pursuing Cheyenne when Liza Reeve's horse stumbled and threw her hard to the ground.

Ellis pulled his pony in and returned to Liza's side. She had lost a lot of blood from the shoulder wound and the arrow was still imbedded in her thigh. The Cheyenne were riding harder now. Liza's pony was dead; its heart had burst. Ellis pulled her up in his arms and helped her to his pony's back, then swung up behind her.

The Cheyenne were only a thousand yards away now and he could hear them yelling. He spurred the broom-tail with a vicious kick in the ribs and sent the exhausted beast at full gallop across the grass, eyes searching for some place where they could stop and make a stand.

There were only three of them, but with an injured Liza on his hands, three Cheyenne born and raised in the high-grass buffalo country were more than enough to contend with. He had his belt of cartridges and the carbine and a Colt. But what he needed most now was a place to fort up and protect his rear.

He urged the slowing pony on to greater speed, but the added weight and the full gallop from the draw had taken a heavy toll of the long-maned pinto. The Cheyenne were within seven hundred yards.

The pony fought its way to the top of a ridge, an outcropping of the sand-hill country of the South Platte, and Ellis saw his stand.

A dried-out pit now in the late June summer, Ellis could see that it was a buffalo wallow and sump when the water was high with the spring rains. Wind, erosion and constant usage by the buffalo had carved out a six-foot overhang beneath the ridge that was squared off in such a manner as to provide protection on three sides and a full view of the plains in front.

He glanced back at the Cheyenne, who saw that he was making for the wallow, and heard them yelling and screaming.

He pushed his pony to the limit and pounded across the dry bed. He slammed to a stop, jerking Liza Reeves down after him, and shoved her in to the back of the overhang.

Still holding the pony by the head rope, Ellis turned to fire at the pursuing braves over the back of the beast, but saw they had pulled to a stop just beyond his range.

And he saw that he would never leave the wallow alive unless he managed in some way to kill the Indians.

He pulled the pony into position and fired a bullet behind the animal's ear. The beast dropped like a stone across the mouth of the cut and Ellis crouched behind it. He steadied the carbine across the dead animal's belly, pulled out the Colt, checked to make sure it was loaded and put it on the ground beside him. The Cheyenne were nowhere to be seen. Ellis guessed that they had circled the wallow and were examining his position from the rear to see if there was any way to reach him from there. Ellis knew that there wasn't, and for a moment he turned his attention to Liza Reeves.

"Stop gaping at my nakedness and get this shaft outa my leg," she said strongly. Her face was a little drawn, beneath the heavy sunburn, but her voice was steady. She handed him the Green River knife she had taken from the dead brave and turned her head away.

On close examination, Ellis saw that the Cheyenne arrow had not penetrated too deeply, only about an inch below the curve of the thigh. The arrowhead had broken

76

off in their flight, and the Texan quickly shaved the shaft to a point to ease the withdrawal.

"This is going to hurt like hell, woman."

"Just pull it out and stop your yammering," she said tartly.

Ellis glanced back at the open sump, and, seeing no sign of the Cheyenne, pulled the shaft out of her thigh. He massaged the wound to make it bleed, and then stripped off his shirt.

"You tend to the savages," she said. "I'll bind this thing up."

"How about your shoulder?"

"That one's all right. It's already dried up in its own blood."

She tore the shirt into several strips and bound her leg tightly. Then she began to bend it at the knee to keep the circulation going and to work out the soreness that was sure to come to the injured muscle.

"We're in a hell of a situation," Ellis said, turning his attention to the face of the cut.

"Ain't near's bad as we was back in that draw," she said quietly. "I guess there wasn't too much I coulda done for ol' Jake noway. He looked pretty gone already. I'm glad they didn't put an arrow in his innards, so he'd lie there and suffer."

Ellis turned. "I never saw anything like it in my life," he said reverently. "You got more Goddam grit in your craw, woman, than any company of Georgia Confeds."

"Turn your head, God damn it," Liza Reeves said angrily. "Lookin' at my nakedness when you have to is one thing, but I'm tryin' to make a skitter-cover outa this shirt and I don't want you watchin' me tie it on."

Ellis could not help but grin. He swept the plains for signs of grass moving unnaturally or against the breath of the wind. He saw nothing, heard nothing.

"All right, you kin look now," Liza said. She had pulled the shirt around her thighs as a diaper and tied the sleeves around her waist.

"As I was sayin'," Ellis began, "you fought like a damned wildcat—"

Her eyes flashed. "Whatcha want me to do? They was gonna kill us, warn't they? You heard what that chile said about stampedin' the bluffer into the camp with us leadin' the shebang—" She stopped short. "So that's what that youngun has in his mind! I thought they was mighty few Goddam Cheyenne in that draw. And then him ridin' off like that."

Ellis nodded grimly. "Probably goin' to stampede the herd, and then attack from the north or east durin' the confusion."

Liza Reeves massaged her thigh. Her face twisted in a grimace of pain. "Ain't goin' to be any easier with all them laborin' men gettin' drunk on their pay tonight, neither."

"And we're pinned down tighter than a cinch strap on a sweatin' mule," Ellis said tightly. "How do you feel?"

"Like fightin'," she said. "We ain't goin' to last long in this wallow. I'm already about to perish to death from thirst."

Ellis turned back to sweep the crust of the sump and, beyond it, the wavering plains grass. It was a sure bet the Cheyenne were behind them and they would be planning. It wasn't likely they would rush them again, sweeping past on their ponies. They would try trickery.

"What would you do," Liza asked, as though she were reading his mind, "if you had two fellows holed up like this? How would you figure it?"

Ellis scratched his chin. "With me bein' a Cheyenne, I'd be pretty good with bow 'n' arrow. I think I'd get over yonder in the high grass over the crust of the wallow hole and fire them shafts—"

"That's all right," Liza said. "Where would you put your horses?"

"I wouldn't put them in back 'cause a stray arrow might get one," Ellis said thoughtfully. "I think I'd hobble them farther east. Where I could keep my eye on them."

"Then let's just wait until we see if that's what they're gonna do," Liza Reeves said and continued to massage her leg.

Ellis watched her, really seeing for the first time her thigh and the full swell of her hard little belly and her rump and the tilt of her breasts against the rough buckskin blouse. He swallowed hard. She was a hell of a lot of woman.

He jerked his head away and stared out over the sump. "You said you was thirsty. I could plug a hole in this pony's vein and get a little blood for you."

She didn't answer.

"Then you ain't very thirsty," he said.

"I seen the way you looked at me then," Liza Reeves said, her eyes flashing. "Don't get no ideas about me."

Ellis flushed. Then he grinned and stared brazenly at her half nudity. "Woman," he said, "there ain't nothin' this side of hell that would keep me from takin' you if I wanted to."

"You just try it and see, cowboy," she said.

"What you got against men?" Ellis asked thoughtfully.

"Nothin'. I guess when I find me a man I'm goin' to have a henhouse full of kids."

"But—"

"But hell! It's gotta be legal. And he's got to be a hell of a lot more man than I've seen around lately." She sniffed and continued to massage her leg.

"I could fill the bill," Ellis said, his eyes searching the grass that showed no sign of the Cheyenne that he knew were out there somewhere.

"What makes you think you'd do for me?" Liza snapped.

"I know it—and you know it," Ellis said confidently.

Liza Reeves tossed her head. "God a'mighty! You're the last man on earth I'd give up to. I'd outshoot you—outhunt you—outrun you—"

"And outtalk me, just like any other woman," Ellis said with a grin. "You don't interest me, lady. And I'll tell you why. When I get me a woman, she ain't only got to wear dresses and act like she was a woman, but she's got to look at me like I was the one and only man in the world."

"Whew! We sure doin' a lot of confessin' in this here wallow. But then, I guess it comes natural with a Texan who rides high on a horse and carries a Colt low."

"I just like to wear my gun handy."

"Too handy. It's killin'-handy."

"Ain't no use talkin' about it any more," Ellis said, somehow a little angry. "I just as soon nuzzle up to a she-bear as try and make shine with you."

Liza tossed her head. "I'd make you forget your ma, boy," she said confidently. "I warn't raised with the Injuns with their free-lovin' ideas with my eyes closed."

"Sure." Ellis nodded. "I figured you'd know a lot—"

"And I ain't been touched, neither!" Liza said flatly. "I'm one hundred per cent woman and the man that gits me is gonna know it, too."

An arrow whistled through the silence of the plains and narrowly missed the opening above the dead pony. The shaft buried itself deep in the animal's rump and quivered there.

Ellis jerked up the carbine and dropped flat to the ground. A second arrow sailed through the air and landed short. A third found the opening, but by this time, Liza Reeves was down flat on the ground beside Ellis and the shaft dug its way into the rear of the cut harmlessly.

"Watch where they're comin' from," Ellis said squinting. "Try to figure out their position."

Hugging the dead horse as closely as possible, Liza Reeves twisted around to find a view of her half of the opening, and, in doing so, had to press her belly, hips and thighs up against Ellis. The Texan gulped and grinned, looking down at her.

"You just keep your mind on business, cowboy," she said.

Three arrows sang through the air; all of them were well aimed and landed in a six-inch circle just below the edge of the pony's back.

"They clustered together straight out," Liza said. "I seen all three of them comin'."

"Same here," Ellis replied. "We'll let them throw three more, then I got an idea."

As if the Cheyenne had heard, three more shafts whistled over the sump, a little higher that the last three, missing the horse altogether and skimming over the top to bury deep in the rear wall of the cut.

"Next volley, you let out a scream."

They waited.

A single arrow, well aimed and moving so fast that they could hardly hear it, skimmed over the top of the horse and sank ten inches into the wall of the cut. Liza let out a blood-curdling scream and began to moan.

"Keep it up," Ellis hissed.

Liza screamed again, this time cutting it off abruptly.

Ellis yelled hoarsely, "Liza—Liza—Liiizzzaaaaa!" He cursed viciously at the Cheyenne for killing her.

"Stick your leg out beyond the edge of the horse. Make 'em think they got you," Ellis whispered. "They wouldn't shoot at a dead leg."

Liza snaked her bad leg out. If they were going to shoot at her, might as well be the one already bunged up, she reasoned.

Ellis began to cry. He wailed and carried on, cursing the Indians he knew were listening.

He slipped the Colt over to Liza. "Get yourself in a position to shoot when they show themselves. And woman, you better make your braggin' come true. You gonna get just about three seconds to plug them braves before they send other arrows into our bodies for good measure."

"You gonna play dead?"

Ellis nodded. "I'm gonna yell, then slump across the top of this hoss, even drop my rifle outside to make 'em think they really got me. More'n likely they'll move in with their bows strung ready to fly that safety arrow, but

82

they'll move in to do it. That's when you gotta throw lead fast and straight."

"All right, I kin see the whole sump now," Liza said, inching her way down to where she had the gun free. She checked the Colt and held it covered by the horse's broomtail that flowed out on the ground.

Three arrows sang over the sump. Two of them dug into the pony and a third thunked into the back of the cut. Ellis let out a death-rattling groan and began to cough and curse. He slumped forward over the dead pony, fully exposed to the sump and the Cheyenne. He dropped his rifle in the dry dust.

He remained still, his skin crawling at the thought of Cheyenne arrows sinking into his head and back. Then he heard Liza cock the colt. He fought hard against an impulse to drop back behind the pony, but he remained still. His face was dry, bone-dry, where only a few minutes before he had been soaked in sweat.

He hard the rustle of the plains grass. Then the Colt barked three times so fast that Ellis could hardly believe the shots came from the same gun.

He jerked up straight, threw himself over the pony and grabbed the rifle. On one knee, he pumped slugs into the three Cheyenne, the force of the bullets hurling the braves back against the crust of the wallow.

The reverberating echoes of the shots were still rolling across the grass when Ellis, joined by Liza, examined the dead bucks.

Liza slipped the Colt into Ellis's holster and stood looking at the Indians. "Mister," she said slowly, "it took guts to play dead in full view of three Cheyenne with arrows strung in their bows."

"I'll go get the horses," Ellis said. He moved away quickly.

When Ellis returned with the three ponies, Liza Reeves had stripped down to the flesh and was preparing to put on a pair of a dead Indian's breeches. As naked as the day she was born, she looked up startled to find Ellis holding the head ropes of the broomtails and grinning at her.

"Turn your head, God damn it!" she said.

"Woman," Ellis said in a heavy drawl, "I just killed more Cheyenne than I ever thought I'd have to—in a fair contest. You don't scare me. And God damn it, I'm lookin'!"

Even from across the sump, Ellis could see Liza Reeves's face turn red beneath the deep tan. Her eyes flashed, but she didn't say another word. Ellis swung to the back of a pony and watched her dress, openly, brazenly, his eyes travelling from the long thighs to the hips, from the firm belly to the full breasts. A hell of a lot of woman, he said to himself. A regular goddam dream of a woman.

Belted and snug in the breeches, Liza pulled on an ornamental vest and laced it up the front to cover her bare bosom. She picked up a bow and slung a quiver of arrows over her shoulder. Limping against the wound in her thigh, she swung up on a pony.

"We'd better light out fast," Ellis said, cutting south to avoid the draw. "Unless we can get help from the camp to come back and clean out those other Cheyenne, there's goin' to be hell to pay with a herd of buffalo stampedin' through the tents."

"Let's go," Liza Reeves said tersely.

Trailing the third pony, they moved off to the south and east, riding hard in the late afternoon sun.

Chapter Six

AT ONE O'CLOCK Liam Kelly began to fret, searching the plains to the west. By this time the Johnny-Jacks had laid four miles of rails, faster than it had ever been put down before. Kelly rode a borrowed horse to the railhead now, ignoring the Jehus' carts hauling the rails.

By two o'clock Kelly really began to worry. He rode back to the tent city, hoping with all his might that Ellis and Jake and Liza Reeves had returned safely with news that his fears were unfounded. He pounded up to a stop before his tent and threw the neck rope to the crippled Jehu who came out to greet him with a grin. "They show up yet, boy?" he demanded.

"Not yet, Mr. Kelly."

"Never mind the horse, lad," Kelly said. "Get over to Watson's and see if they've stopped there for a drink. Then come find me at the general's."

The boy nodded and hobbled away as quickly as he could on the make-shift crutch. Kelly turned toward the general's tent.

"General's moved to his caboose, Kelly," Billy Brighton told him. The ex-major was sweating over a drafting board. "Any word from Jake, or from Miss Reeves? Or from the cowboy?"

"Not a sign of them," Kelly said.

Brighton pursed his lips. "You better get over and tell the general. That detachment of soldiers that came down on the pay train's due to return to Omaha tonight. And some of the regulars with the camp are going back on leaves, the replacements coming in next week. If there's anything coming up, we're going to be mighty shorthanded."

Kelly hurried out of the engineers' tent, half ran to the rails, flagged a Jehu and climbed aboard. Flying down the side of the rails with a load of cross ties, Kelly was deposited outside the general's caboose and climbed aboard.

One half of the car was given over to sleeping and living quarters for the man in charge of putting through the Union Pacific. The other half resembled a small arsenal, littered with drafting boards, rolls of surveyors' maps and engineering gear of every kind.

The congressmen were still bending the general's ear when Kelly swung up on the car and pushed in.

He caught the general's eye. The general knew at a glance that his big roving bucko was worried. He bent a finger at Kelly and moved away from the others and into his private quarters.

The door closed behind them and he turned to face the big man. "What is it, Kelly?"

"No word, General," Kelly said heavily. "Still nothin' specific. I sent a scout out 'fore noon and he was trailed by that young woman, Jake Reeves's sister. I haven't heard from either of them. Nor Jake, either. I don't like it, General."

The general closed his eyes and pressed his fingers to the bridge of his nose. "Want me to send out a detachment of soldiers?"

Kelly shook his head. "No, sir, but Major Brighton just told me that the pay train guards and some regulars were headed back to Omaha tonight on the return supply train. If we could keep them in camp, it might help—in case anythin' happens."

86

"If anything happens, Kelly," the general said. He pointed to the door. "There are three congressmen outside, and each one of them is intent on hamstringing this whole operation. They hated President Lincoln's guts and they'd just love to go back to Washington and raise hell. I can't go into the whole political-financial intrigue of the building of this railroad now, Kelly, but unless you can give me concrete assurances that Goose Face and a war party are in the area, I can't ask the detachment of regulars going home on leave—or the specials who came out on the pay train—to stay. It all adds up to money, Kelly. Those congressmen outside would like nothing better than to go back and raise hell with Andy Johnson for going ahead with Lincoln's plan of building a continental railroad."

"There'd be a lot more hell to pay, sir," Kelly said angrily, "if that renegade devil swooped down on us, and only half of our soldiers—"

"Soldiers! My God, Kelly, do you realize that nearly a fifth of the men working on this road are ex-soldiers! And we have the guns and ammunition to tear Goose Face and any war party to bits."

"I want to avoid an attack altogether, sir. I'll see if I can't get somebody else to ride out as scout—"

"I'll give you six men," the general said. "I'll put them directly under you."

Kelly nodded, his jaw tight. "All right, General."

* * *

The soldiers, mounted, listened impatiently to Kelly instructing the sergeant. To a man, they thought Kelly crazy as a loon for suggesting that a party of a hundred or so Indians would dare to attack the railhead. They

87

were annoyed at being ordered out on a hot afternoon to ride in search of a scout who had probably taken a jug of Watson's whisky along with him and was sleeping off a drunk, or to trail after a cowboy and a leather-tough plains girl with a hot eye for each other.

"I want you to split up into three parties," Kelly ordered. "Ride north and south of the buffalo, with one of you going in a wide circle well out from the others. The two scouts and the girl are out there somewhere, and even if you don't see any Cheyenne, I want you to bring them back in."

Surly and ill-tempered, the troopers turned their horses west and out of camp, in no hurry to ride hard across the baking plains grass. Kelly watched them leave, wishing under his breath that he could crack their heads together. There was nothing for him to do now but wait. No, he would not just sit around. He would go out to the railhead and keep the Johnny-Jacks moving. Kelly did not have to be told that there was fire in the air that hot Saturday afternoon, and that the Johnny-Jacks were pounding their way to more track footage laid in a single day than had ever been put down before. He swung his big frame into the saddle of his borrowed horse and galloped out to the railhead.

* * *

Goose Face sat under the shade of a cottonwood tree and tore into a fresh liver just taken from the warm body of a buffalo calf. Around him, hardly visible in a grove of trees well east of the rail camp, his small army of dedicated white-haters waited with him.

The Cheyenne leader bit into the liver and let the warm blood run down his chin and drip onto his bare chest. His eyes studied the middle distance, his gaze

88

moody and thoughtful. It had not always been like this for the young renegade.

Goose Face's mind drifted back to the time when he was but a child in the tepee, curling up in a buffalo robe on the cold winter nights and staring into the fire. His father, a tall handsome brave with many coups, would stroke his knife on a stone and speak softly to his mother. The young boy would listen to stories of battles with the Sioux to the west and north, and of running engagements with the Arapaho and Crow. And tales of the great hunts when braves from all the lodges would follow the chief down into the great plains for buffalo.

The young boy liked it best when the hunters returned, their horses laden with dripping beef and thick bloody stacks of buffalo hides. The squaws in every lodge would turn out to greet the bucks and a big feast would follow. Then the squaws would begin preparing the robes for new tepee skins, removing the old ones that were then smoked and dried soft for making moccasins and leggings for the brave hunters.

Soft-and-Running-Deer had waited impatiently for the day when he would become a brave and sit with the other braves in the council and make wise decisions. He worked hard under his father's guiding hand, learning to read trail signs, to ride a pony, and to hunt in the forests and the streams of the Dakotas when parties would forage north.

The eighteen-year-old Cheyenne leader remembered the maid Many Blossoms, who had grown up with him and for whom he had fought his first fight with knives when he was only fourteen. He had sworn that when he returned from his first single hunt, with the hair of an enemy, thereby declared a true brave of the Cheyenne ready to take his place at the councils, he would take Many Blossoms for his squaw. His father, Buffalo Eye, ant the father of the maid, Big Moon, both had looked favorably on this. And the girl herself had shown that she desired the young son of Buffalo Eye.

The fight had been with an older, heavier and more experienced Cheyenne who had offered robes and other gifts to the father of Many Blossoms in exchange for the young girl. Soft-and-Running-Deer had promised as many robes and as many gifts — in time — and the father of Many Blossoms had accepted his promise, but the decision had to be fought out between the young growing buck and the seasoned brave.

They had met alone on the plains, both riding out to a deserted place and facing each other over knives and tomahawks. Their fight had lasted two hours and, in the end, Soft-and-Running-Deer returned with seventeen knife wounds and the hair of his enemy. At fourteen he had been made a full brave. He sat in the councils and respect was paid when the chief himself listened as he recounted his one coup before the tribe.

On advice from his father, the young brave had delayed taking Many Blossoms as his squaw until he had paid for her, fulfilling his debt of buffalo robes and other gifts to the maid's father.

As his eyes studied the distant fires of the railhead camp in the sinking afternoon sun, Goose Face remembered that he had just finished paying off his debt to Big Moon for the maid when the long knives had struck their village. He had seen his mother, his father, and Many Blossoms shot to death before he himself had been cut down by one of the soldiers.

The scene of horror filled the young renegade's eyes as if it were happening that instant.

He dropped the calf liver and jerked up straight. He screamed, throwing his head back, and let the fury of his hate escape from his throat. He began to dance. He writhed and jerked, brandishing his knife in one hand and his carbine in the other. Soon other members of his party began to dance, too, one brave beating out the deadening rhythm on a hollow log. They coursed around into a rough circle and screamed and shook their bodies, and let their hate for the white men take possession of them completely.

* * *

By four-thirty, when the shadows reached long across the plains, the Johnny-Jacks had laid nearly seven miles of track.

By four-thirty the detachment of soldiers sent out by Liam Kelly had formed up in the draw where Liza had performed her own personal massacre on the Cheyenne, and were cut down by the remaining braves. The soldiers fought back valiantly, but the Cheyenne were angry and their arrows were straight and heavily bowed. The soldiers died without killing one of the enemy.

At four-thirty Ellis and Liza Reeves stopped in the protection of overgrown prairie grass to attend to Liza's leg. It was beginning to pain badly, and had continued to bleed. Ellis started a fire with gunpowder taken from precious cartridges and heated the Green River knife. While Liza bit down hard on the lead of a cartridge, he cauterized the wound, fighting his own rising gorge as the stench of burning flesh reached his nostrils.

By four-thirty the sun had dropped into the place on the horizon named by Goose Face as the signal for the

91

stampede of the herd into the rail camp. The remaining Cheyenne braves moved to the ponies recaptured after their dash from the draw.

And far to the east of the camp, Goose Face and his party of braves continued to dance their ceremonial prelude to death.

The dancing stopped at the commanding scream of Goose Face. The braves stood rooted in their tracks, listening. From the west rolled a great roar of thunder.

Goose Face dropped to the ground and put his ear against the earth. In the ground he could hear the pounding of thousands of hoofs; he thought he could hear the screams and cries of pain of the white men and their squaws and their little ones as the great herd advanced toward the tent community.

Goose Face jumped up. He raised his tomahawk and carbine over his head, and cried out the order. In a frenzy the braves raced for their horses and, at the heels of Goose Face, struck west across the great plains and toward the railhead.

Chapter Seven

NATHAN ELLIS and Liza Reeves were within a mile of the tent city when they heard the thunder of the buffalo hoofs. They stopped still in the high grass and stared in fascination and wonder and more than a little fear at the herd pounding across the plains. The dust rose over the backs of the huge plains beasts in a thick cloud that nearly blotted out the sun. Her leg smarting and aching from the hot knife, but better now that the bleeding had stopped, Liza Reeves kicked her pony hard and rode for the camp alongside Ellis, both of them throwing backward glances at the herd and at the furious, swirling cloud of dust.

Liam Kelly was the first to spot the advancing herd of buffalo. He thought at first the dust cloud was a sandstorm blowing up, or perhaps the advance of a cyclone. At first he mistook the beat of the hoofs for thunder from cloudheads.

The Johnny-Jacks stopped their work, ignored the bawling buckos and turned to stare at the western sky. And when they heard the roar of the hoofs, work stopped altogether at the railhead.

Liam Kelly whipped his pony around and rode out beyond the railhead some hundred yards, away from the jabbering men so that he could listen. His big face paled. He jerked his pony around and flailed the animal at top speed back to the railhead.

"Buffalo stampede!" he roared above the din. "Get back! Get back!"

The men did not have to be warned twice. They dropped their tools and scurried for the work train and the three flatcars. The engineers and firemen worked together pouring wood into the firebox, building the steam up even as the men were climbing aboard. Ties, rails, horses and mules were abandoned in the mad flight.

The cars began to roll before the last of the men were aboard and these were helped onto the flatcars by others who jerked them clear of the ground.

The balloon stack belched smoke and tongues of raw flame as the train began to back up toward the camp, the men shouting at each other above the roar of the locomotive.

Kelly pounded alongside the train as it backed toward the camp.

Further to the south, Liza Reeves and Ellis saw excited men, women and children gathering at the outer edges of the community to stare in wonder at the hurtling supply train.

With a sigh of relief, Kelly spotted Ellis and Liza and spurred his pounding animal at an angle to meet them. The three riders drew up to a stop within a few yards of the outermost tent.

"It's a stampede!" Kelly roared.

"I know it's a stampede," Ellis replied. "It's Goose Face and his men doing it."

"Where's Jake?"

"Dead, with a Cheyenne arrow in his head," Liza said, and then groaned as the pain in her leg stabbed viciously.

"You hurt?"

"Nothin' to holler about, Mr. Kelly. But you going' to have a hell of a mess if you don't get these women and chillun outa this camp before them bluffers come streakin' in."

"Is there a chance to turn them?"

Ellis shook his head. "I don't know, but there's a party makin' up that's goin' to try." He pointed toward the camp, where Johnny-Jacks, soldiers, Jehus and anyone that could find a horse and a gun of some sort had begun to form a rough group.

"Let's go," Liza Reeves said and started to spur her pony around.

Ellis grabbed at the head rope and hung on tight. "No, you don't!"

"Leggo of that, you meat-headed idiot!"

"You're going over to the doctorin' tent and get that leg and shoulder fixed up properly."

"Who you think you're orderin' around!" Liza Reeves exploded, trying to tear her pony away from Ellis's grip.

Ellis roared. He opened his mouth and bellowed, "I'm orderin' you, God damn it! Even if I have to get off this hoss and whip you and hog-tie you to a tent pole, you're gonna stay back here with the others!"

Liza Reeves blinked, stunned at the sudden ferocity in a man who had shown himself to be brave enough, but not spectacularly strong. "Now git!" Ellis snapped. "If them bluffer do get through us and we can't turn 'em away from the camp, there's goin' to be hell to pay—and clear-headed folks needed to care of the women and kids!"

Liam Kelly had remained silent, but now he nodded in agreement. "He's right, miss. You'll be more help back here if we can't turn that herd."

"Let's go!" Ellis shouted and jerked his pony around and looked straight west after the nearly two hundred riders picking up speed in a headlong rush to meet the buffalo. Kelly turned his mount and raced after the others.

Liza Reeves, in spite of her leg wound and the imminent danger of the buffalo herd, could not help but blink and grin at the departing Nathan Ellis. He sure was a hell of a lot of man, she thought. Just about nigh perfect.

She trotted her pony into the edge of the tents, flushing even now at the way Nathan Ellis had looked at her naked body while she was pulling on the dead Indian's breeches and vest.

* * *

The railroad men pounded at full gallop directly into the path of the onrushing buffalo, now no more than seven or eight miles ahead of them. Like a black tide, the beasts swarmed in an ever-widening front until they stretched for nearly two miles across the plains. The riders held their breath as they saw the black wave engulf the railhead, tearing the carts and wagons left behind into splinters. Hundreds, thousands of buffalo, many of them weighing almost a full ton, pounded at express-train speed in a wide swath across the grass, without sign that they would ever be stopped until their hearts burst or their spindly legs broke beneath their weight.

At a signal from an old line sergeant riding at the point of the mob of men, they unlimbered their guns and prepared to fire.

"Keep together!" the old sergeant roared above the din, and wiggled his arms. "Spread out and you're done for!"

Somehow the galloping men understood and closed ranks.

Ellis and Kelly rode side by side, the Texan wishing he had a solid Texas saddle beneath him rather than having

96

to depend on his legs to keep him on the pony. Kelly had gripped his reins in one hand, while with his free hand he brandished the heavy old Colt. Ellis still had the carbine and had reloaded long before. His Colt was slapping his legs and he cursed himself for having forgotten to tie the holster down. Afraid that the piece would fall out, the Texan shoved the gun into his waistband and closed ranks with the determined, frightened railroad party.

They would rather have been anyplace else this side of hell than riding into a buffalo stampede. There was the promise of a sure death of some, and injury and pain for many. But they went on anyway; hard and fast, straight for the sea of maddened beasts packed so tightly together it was barely possible to distinguish one animal from another.

They were a scant three miles from the herd now. The line sergeant held up a hand and the band of men ground to a stop. Ellis knew what the old soldier had in mind and he agreed. The buffalo still had a good run before they would hit the camp and if the horses were to be expected to run much more they had to have a rest, however short.

Ellis scanned the surging buffalo for some signs of a leader—an old bull, or a group of bulls—but he could see none. The dust was beginning to reach them now. The wind had shifted and swung the cloud before the onrushing animals.

The men held their ponies in tightly, checking and re-checking their guns as they waited for the sergeant, who was conferring loudly with Kelly, to give them instructions.

"They still got a run before they reach the camp," the sergeant said, keeping his eyes on the beasts all the while, "and if we could turn 'em just a bit—it looks to me like they're favoring the north—we might get 'em to go past the main body of the camp."

"Do we ride into 'em, Sergeant?" a young Jehu asked.

"You do, boy, and you'll never ride out!" the sergeant bawled.

"You ride in front of them, son," Ellis said. "And you keep in front of them, shooting behind you, trying to kill the leaders."

"They're getting close, Sarge!" a voice bellowed from the crowd.

"All right, men! Let's go to hell for supper! Eeeoooyoooow!"

The buffalo were a scant thousand yards away from them now, and the red eyes of the animals were easily distinguishable by the time the riders had whipped their horses around and begun to ease along, looking over their shoulders to watch the buffalo gain on them. Gradually they picked up speed as the buffalo came closer, and then some of the men began to fire into the herd. Ellis saw a buffalo drop and saw several others stumble over the fallen beast, but the tide merely swarmed around them, stamping them to death. The noise was deafening. More shots rang out, then more and more, and Ellis saw one, then three, then ten, then twenty of the buffalo fall. Still those behind came pushing on.

A Jehu's horse stumbled in a gopher hole and threw the boy to the grass. The rider got up and raced for his horse, gained it and was in the saddle when the herd reached him, the leading bulls goring the horse and throwing the Jehu into the air. The boy disappeared beneath the hoofs.

Another rider went down and was trampled beneath the hoofs. More and more buffalo were killed as lead from nearly two hundred guns poured into the outer edge of the herd.

Ellis had been riding hard, his legs locked on the ribs and shoulders of his pony, firing coolly and carefully into the herd, when he noticed he was being overtaken on his right. He grabbed the head rope of his pony, urged it on and then dared a glance to his right. They had made an effective hole in the center of the line, but the buffalo were filling it from the sides. Though dozens dropped before the wall of fire, the gigantic herd did not hesitate in its rush forward.

Their mounts were tiring now and Ellis saw one and then another of the railroad men thrown to the ground as a horse's heart burst or a gopher hole or sand pit trapped a hoof. Ellis's own pony faltered and he thought he would go down, but the sturdy little animal picked up its gallop and was soon back in stride racing before the oncoming buffalo.

They were riding hard on the camp now. Ellis could see the frenzy of activity around the tents as women and children scurried back out of the way. There was a sharp, shrill noise and Ellis could not identify it for a moment. Then he realized that it was the steam whistle of the engine. He could see the train pulling out. Every spare car on the temporary siding had been coupled and it now swarmed with women, children and men.

His attention was jerked back to his left where seven riders went down together as if their horses had been tied to a rope and the rope had run out. A sand pit, not very wide and not very long, had trapped the hoofs of their ponies. Ellis saw them and their horses crushed to a pulp by the maddened beasts.

Suddenly his hands burned and he realized that he had fired his carbine until it was nearly red-hot. The flesh of the palm on his left hand was blistered and torn, but he gripped against the pain and continued to fire back into the wall of the heard.

Then, from the center of the tent city, Ellis saw two dozen soldiers appear, riding hard and fast on fresh horses straight into the advancing herd. He shouted for them to get back, to turn around and run with the herd, by they did not appear to hear and charged straight into the rumbling black sea of buffalo.

Suddenly there was a tremendous explosion, then another and another. Then more—again and again explosions shattered the air and smoke and dust and splinters flew high. More explosions followed. Ellis saw the soldiers throwing sticks of dynamite into the on-rushing herd of buffalo.

He did not realize that this pony had stopped, or that the other riders had pulled up at the very edge of the tent city and were watching along with him.

The line of beasts wavered, and then there was a sudden swing away on two sides, and as the buffalo swung, the soldiers moved along the outer edges of the herd tossing more sticks to keep them running.

Ellis watched in fascination, not conscious of his nearly raw hand, not conscious of anything really as he saw the soldiers blast the tide into two streams, turning the buffalo around, driving one stream north and the other south.

For forty-five minutes the solders blasted the beasts into submission. For nearly an hour they surged up to the very edge of the tent community, facing continuous fire from more than five hundred guns, in addition to the explosive charges.

When the last beast had swung to the right and the dust of the plains had blown away, as far as the eye could see the grass was bent and steaming. As if a fantastic wind had hailed stones to the ground, the plains lay trampled and churned into a dry field of death. Great black mounds of buffalo were piled at the very steps of the tent community. Parts of buffalo lay everywhere: the animals had been literally torn to pieces by the charges of dynamite. And farther back, every Johnny-Jack and soldier knew, were the bodies of friends and working mates, stamped irrevocably into the dry Nebraska plains, so thoroughly torn to pieces by thousands of hoofs that when riders went out in search of possible survivors they would not even find so much as a boot.

* * *

Hardly a moment after the stampeding buffalo had been turned away, and the other riders were slipping exhausted from their horses, there came another attack on the tent city from the east.

Goose Face and his hundred followers swarmed up over the hillock eastward of the tents and, screaming war cries, charged straight for the heart of the railhead camp.

The emergency train filled with women and children was blocked a half-mile away by twenty of the braves who had led spare horses onto the tracks and hobbled them there, a bloody sacrifice to prevent any of the whites from escaping.

A third of Goose Face's warriors broke away from the main party and began firing arrows point-blank into the loaded train. The wails and screams of women and children broke out over the late afternoon plains.

Hasty fire was returned by the few men and women aboard who had guns, while others labored to remove the dead and injured carcasses of the screaming horses from the tracks. The engineer had not hesitated to plow

101

his powerful balloon-stack hundred-tonner into the animals, praying that the engine would not be thrown from the tracks.

The wheels had held, a miracle on this day when Providence had seemed to abandon the railroad men and their families.

Soldiers dropped like dead flies before the rain of arrows thrown by the circling Cheyenne, but the horses were removed from the track and the engine throttle shoved wide open, the high wheels slipping and sliding in the blood before catching hold and picking up speed. When the train had succeeded in pulling away from the attackers, the Indians fell away and turned their attention to the camp city itself—where Goose Face and his braves were already wreaking havoc.

The attack was timed so perfectly, the thrust and vengeance of the Indians so violent, that the defenders of the camp reeled back, suffering heavy losses.

Goose Face knew that the white men expected the Indians to attack, circle, and withdraw. He saw them trying to form a hard core of fire power in a large, devastated area strewn with fallen tents. He screamed to his men to follow, and those nearest him swerved their ponies around and galloped after their young leader.

Goose Face plowed straight into the thick of the fire, scattering the railroad men and soldiers with the fury of his unexpected attack. Again and again, he whirled and pounded into the middle of the group until the power of its concentrated fire disintegrated to lone bullets from men forted up behind canvas spills and baggage.

The raid could be counted as a success, but Goose Face had sworn himself to kill the white men until death alone prevented him from drawing a bow.

102

The defenders of the camp, the horsemen who had pounded out to meet and race before the buffalo herd, were now back in the saddle. The enraged Irishmen, the ex-Confederates, the Jehus, the soldiers, the scattering of gun-slingers and drunks, the engineers and graders, the entire corps that had come out here to build a railroad that would link a continent, roared back against the sudden rain of death Goose Face had poured down on them.

The general's caboose had been brought up and guns were distributed to any who could point and fire. Tarts from the grog tents, missionaries on their way west, the injured and bedridden in medical tents, were given guns and cartridge belts. Two hundred, three hundred, four hundred guns began to answer Goose Face, death for death.

The Cheyenne party continued to thrash and fight, not bothering to reload, but firing until their guns were empty, then—hanging low to the ground—they snatched up fresh guns from the dead or wounded. The finest horsemen in the world, the Cheyenne, showed the hated whites that day what a hundred furious savages could do to the order and plans of civilized men. Again and again the ponies of the Indians were shot out from beneath them, and again and again the savages would remount either one of the railhead's own horses, or an animal of a dead comrade.

Like a swarm of maddened hornets, the Cheyenne attackers broke up the tent city. The stench of powder, scorched flesh and burning canvas filled the air.

The defense was dug in now. The whites were not going to die easily, at least not without taking their toll of the attackers. But Goose Face, seeing that his men were being cut to ribbons, rode directly to a cookfire and lit a buffalo-grease-soaked torch. He screamed his orders to the remaining braves, who followed him, dipped their torches into the fire and sailed them at the tops of the largest tents.

In a matter of minutes, twenty tents were blazing furiously, and thick black columns of smoke were billowing to the twilight sky. With another scream, Goose Face signaled his men to retreat. Followed by less than ten of his original party, the white-masked warrior whipped his pony to the south and west, after the buffalo. Behind him, he left over a hundred dead, two hundred wounded, a raging fire and destruction on a scale equal to the bloodiest of the fights between the white and red men on the western plains.

* * *

The furious heat, the searing flames that consumed the canvas tents in minutes, were not the concern of Nathan Ellis. The Texan had wrapped his raw palm in a bandanna and fought back against the attackers with pure violence. Not since the war had this tall man felt such rage fill his throat. Twice he had sighted on Goose Face himself, and twice he had pulled a hammer down on a dead cartridge.

The moment Ellis saw Goose Face stoop to light his torch and order the others to follow, the Texan had known the Indian was about to withdraw. He ran to a frightened horse hobbled to a tent stake and, yelling to Kelly, who had fought beside him during the whole attack, was astride the animal when the Cheyenne leader broke away from the fight.

Kelly saw it too and, shouting for Johnny-Jacks to follow him, began jerking at snorting horses and leaping for the bridles of those that had bolted from the roaring fires.

The Indians were about three thousand yards away when a party of five white men broke from the scatter of tents. Ellis's face was grim, streaked with sweat and blood. As he pounded after the small band of surviving Cheyenne, Ellis knew he would not stop until he had killed Goose Face. His mind was filled with scenes of horror he would not forget until the day he died. Without realizing it, he had pulled ahead of the others and was now five hundred yards closer to the Indians, but the ponies of the braves were stronger and gradually they pulled away from the pursuing enemy.

They rode at dead heat for an hour. They rode until their horses were white with lather and trembling from the beat of their hearts. The white men were forced to slow down and watch the dust of the braves gradually disappear into the ridge country of the South Platte.

Kelly pulled up to a stop. "We'll never get him now," he said. He nodded to the western sky. The red had disappeared from the heavens and the plains twilight, short-lived and false, was on them. "It'll be dark before you know it. We'd better get back to the railhead and see what we can do."

"I ain't turnin' back, Mr. Kelly," a soft voice said behind him. Kelly turned to see a grime-covered Slocum.

"I'm goin' to get that Injun," Ellis said flatly. "Tonight, or tomorrow, or next week or next month—if it takes me the rest of my goddam life—I ain't stoppin' till I get me that Injun."

Slocum nudged his horse and walked it beside Ellis. "Well, you got yourself a pardner."

"You goin' back, Kelly?" Ellis asked.

"I don't want to," Kelly said, looking ahead into the distance. "But there's repair work to be done. Monday morning at sunup, the Johnny-Jacks will be puttin' down rail or I'll know the reason why."

Ellis exploded. "You no-good goddam Irish bastard!" he roared. "Men, women and children have been killed today. Good men, fine women and their children—and that heathen Injun is the reason—and all you can think of is buildin' a railroad!"

Kelly met Ellis's gaze. "Mr. Ellis," he said heavily, "there ain't nothin' this side of hell goin' to stop this rail-road from gettin' built. A hundred—two hundred—a thousand! What does it mean when—"

Ellis jerked his pony around. "Let's go," he said to Slocum.

Kelly and the others watched the two riders head out into the black of the onrushing night.

"They don't need us," Kelly said. "We'd just be in the way." He pulled his pony around. "Let's get back, you muckrakers!" he bellowed. "We've got work to do before we can start buildin' our railroad Monday mornin'."

Chapter Eight

HOW YOU GONNA TRAIL them Indians in the dark, Mr. Ellis?"

Ellis did not reply. He extended his hand sideways and found Slocum's arm. He pressed it tightly.

It was close to nine P.M. Ellis thought his body would break from fatigue. His back ached, his head ached and his eyes burned from his stretch in the sun earlier that day. His left hand was useless to him and he held it inside his shirt. For a long time now he had been biting down on a lead bullet, fighting back the agony in his body. He could not remember ever being so tired or so full of pain in so many places at one time in his whole life.

For more than two hours they had been heading due south, hitting the ridge country, listening to the plains wolves howl. There wasn't any moon and Ellis breathed a prayer of thanks for that. The ponies were tired, but Ellis was glad to be riding in a saddle again after spending so much time bareback on a broomtail. The grass was not as high out here as back near the railroad and he was grateful for that, too. Goose Face could not lie in wait too easily and ambush them along the trail.

For some time now, Slocum had been insistent in his question. Ellis, in spite of his pain, had to grin at the young Southerner who could not understand how Ellis was trailing the Cheyenne party in the dark. He had not had a chance to tell Slocum that there was no trail to follow in the black night, but that he was riding south to a place at which he felt sure Goose Face would stop. Even after a war party, Ellis knew that the Cheyenne would be reluctant to travel all night. It had been just as tough a day for Goose face as it had been for Ellis in certain respects, and the tall Texan knew the broomtails the Cheyenne were riding would be just as tired as his own. Somewhere up ahead, Ellis remembered, there was a small creek that fed into the Platte. He was not as familiar with the country as he would have liked to be at the moment, but in his early-morning scout he had spotted the signs of gulleys and dry washes and small gulches running off in a varied pattern, but in the same general direction.

Ellis was staking time and his life on the chance that Goose Face and his men would be camped near that creek, somewhere ahead of them, out in the darkness.

A little further on they hit an eight-foot dry wash and dropped into it. Their horses hoofs were soundless in the powdery sand bed and the further they moved south, angling a little to the west now, the wider the bed became. Ellis began to sniff the air and watch the head of his animal closely. He knew the horses would catch the scent of water before he would and from then on, they would have to move with extreme caution.

They had been riding for another twenty minutes when Ellis felt his pony twist its head slightly and stir beneath him. He pulled back and touched Slocum on the arm. "We leave the horses here," he said. "There's a creek up ahead."

"You know this country?"

"The horses smelled water. I'm bettin' Goose Face is camped somewhere along that creek."

Slocum grunted, and both men eased out of the saddle. "Check your guns," Ellis said.

"I only got two."

"That's all you can shoot at one time, ain't it?"

"Not when I get mad," Slocum said seriously." I'm a hell of a man with guns when I get mad."

"You'll have plenty of time for that later, if Goose Face is where I think he is."

Ellis checked his own Colt and an Army rifle he had used during the attack on the camp. He slung a bandoleer of cartridges over his shoulder, noted that half of them were gone and turned to Slocum. "You got a knife?"

"An old Spanish hog-sticker. You figure you'll need to do some cuttin'? I'm hell with a man when I gotta use my hog-sticker."

In the dark Ellis felt Slocum press the blade into his hand. He drew in a breath. It was nearly eighteen inches long, double-edged and perfectly balanced. "Can you throw that thing?"

"Sink it ten inches in anything I can see."

"You might not be able to see very well."

"Anything I can smell, too."

They hobbled the horses to the roots of a brush thicket and began to move down the bed of the wash.

* * *

Goose Face knew that there were riders behind him. Until the last light of the day, he had watched his trail carefully for signs of dust and, though the rise was smaller, indicating that some of the riders had turned back, he knew at nightfall that he was still being pursued.

He was unmoved. It would just mean more white blood to spill into the plains sands. He made his camp carefully on the north side of the creek, ordered his men to rest, staked out the horses and posted guards. Though the remaining braves were both angry and sorry that their band had been reduced, they knew that they had slain many long beards and, though tired, they ate jerky and recited their many coups counted that day.

Goose Face stretched out on the bank of the creek and stared at the stars. That he had lost so many of his men did not mean anything to him. That he himself had escaped death held no meaning for him either. He had been reduced to a life dedicated to killing the long beards by the mutilation of his face. Among his own men there were many who could not stand to look at his face. And the one time he had tried to take a squaw into a willow-reed bed by the water, she had bitten him on the arm and fled.

He lay, flat, his body relaxing, his mind on the riders who were following him. He got up without a sound, not looking at the other braves, took his bow and half a dozen arrows, his knife and his tomahawk and slipped quietly downstream.

He moved a hundred feet and stopped to listen. Then he moved on another hundred feet before cutting up the bank through a thicket of brush and out onto the open plains. He stopped dead still and listened to the wind.

He heard nothing.

He moved on without a sound and made a wide circle around the outer edge of his camp, stopping frequently to listen. When he was near the creek again, he heard a noise. He froze into absolute stillness, holding his breath and listening to the wind.

He heard it again, to his left.

He dropped to the ground and began to crawl back toward the creek.

* * *

Ellis and Slocum sat hunched in the middle of a thicket and watched the Indians across the creek, vaguely visible in the starlight.

They had crossed the water a thousand yards below the camp, and had heard the movements of the Indian ponies. Working their way up carefully and slowly, they were now in a position to watch the camp from across the river.

"I can see every one of 'em." Slocum whispered.

"Wait until they go to sleep."

"Where you think them guards will be?"

"Closer to the horses," Ellis said. "They'll not only watch for us, but keep wolves away from the ponies."

"How many braves can you see from here?"

Slocum counted under his breath. "I make out eight."

"Any of them with a face painted white?"

"Nope."

"He could have washed his face," Ellis said, but he didn't believe it.

"How long we gonna sit here watchin' them jokers eat? Why don't we just cut down on 'em? I could get half a dozen before they could wet their britches."

Goose Face must be among them, Ellis thought. He's just as tired as they are and he's got guards posted. "I think," Ellis said quietly, pulling the Army rifle up to his shoulder, "that we'd better take what we've got and leave the rest till later."

"Now you're talkin', man," Slocum said. "Let's divide these Injuns up evenly. See that bunch over to one side—looks like five or six of them sittin' cross-legged eatin'? Well, them's mine."

Ellis agreed and sighted on the remaining braves who were seated closer to the edge of the water.

"Fire slow and straight," Slocum said under his breath. "Learned a lot in the great conflict between the states, but I learned most about killin' men. Shoot straight and aim well. That way you don't waste bullets, besides which you don't usually get a second shot at the same fellow."

"I don't know how we lost the war with you fightin' for us," Ellis said dryly.

"I got into the fracus just a little late. Things was already turned bad by then."

"All right," Ellis said. "On the count of three." He paused. Then, "One—two—*three!*"

Slocum proved himself a dead shot, and he followed his own rule of taking aim slowly and shooting straight. Across the creek the Indians leaped up, shouting, and made the mistake that sealed their doom. They scrambled for their guns instead of seeking cover.

There was method and a deadly neat accuracy to Ellis's and Slocum's shots. Four of Slocum's Indians were shot in the head, a fifth in the heart, and the sixth right between the eyes.

Ellis had used three more shots to get his four Indians, but they were just as dead.

When the echoes were gone, they heard the pounding of hoofs. It was the posted guard making his escape.

112

"Goddam if this wasn't like takin' care of the little animals Paw used to send me out after. Used to whale the tar outa me if I messed up a squirrel with a gut shot—"

There was a heavy, sickening *thunk* of an arrow sinking into flesh, and Slocum slumped forward without a sound, a Cheyenne shaft quivering in the base of his skull.

Ellis dropped to the ground and crawled as fast as he could toward the water. He splashed along the shore, found an opening in the brush and moved up cautiously toward the high edge of the bank nearer the open plains.

There was a bloodcurdling scream. And then another, and a crashing through the underbrush back where Ellis had left Slocum. Ellis fired rapidly into the brush and then charged back in again, the rifle empty, the Colt bucking in his right hand.

He stumbled to where Slocum lay and with a curse felt the bloody, raw head of the dead man Goose Face had scalped.

Goose Face screamed again. "I kill you, too! I kill you, too!"

Ellis shoved the Colt into his holster and searched around Slocum's body for the knife. He found it. "Goose Face!" he bellowed. "I'm goin' to kill you with my bare hands! You hear! I'm goin' to take your hair! And your ears, Goose Face!"

"You die!" Goose Face screamed. "You come, you die, too!"

* * *

The two men were silent, both of them straining their ears against the sighing breeze and examining the rustle of the grass and brush. They listened to the murmur of the water in the creek and each waited for the other to make the move that would betray his position.

113

Goose Face gripped his bow. He had three shafts left and the advantage was all his, he knew. A lifetime of silent panther like movement on the plains; a lifetime of listening to the south winds blowing up from the west Texas and Kansas plains; an intuition grounded to the stalking hunt.

Goose Face strung an arrow. He lay in the deep grass beyond the edge of the creek. He had gone there when he retired from the thicket, placing his back to the plains and watching for the shadow of his foe to rise against the star-studded sky. He would catch any movement, if not by sight, then by sound. There were a hundred messages for him to read if the white man did more than breathe.

He lay still and listened. The breeze sighed and wafted the leaves on the cottonwood near the creek. An old she-wolf howled and even the whimper of her whelp touched the ears of the savage lying in wait with the practiced patience of the hunter.

* * *

Nathan Ellis's hand pained him so much that he had to stifle a cry of agony. He lay belly-down in the soft dry sand in the bottom of a bed that was still warm from the afternoon heat. His breath was heavy and labored and all the more difficult as he tried to control it. He knew that his enemy was deadly and brave, arrogant and reckless, and fighting in his own country. Ellis was conscious that all the advantages were on the side of the savage somewhere out ahead of him in the darkness.

His left hand would not close, but he did not really need it. His right hand curled around the butt of his Colt. He rammed Slocum's hog-sticker into the empty holster — the blade's naked point just shying away from his leg.

114

The Indian, Ellis knew, would stalk him like a hunter. He would follow all the rules of the plainsman in the hunt for the beast. But Ellis was not a dumb thing to be outwitted. He would not bolt from fear or try to overcome his enemy with brute strength. If Goose Face was going to hunt him like an animal, then Ellis knew he must do everything an animal would do—until the moment the hunter exposed himself in that split second before the kill. In that second, Ellis's cunning as a thinking man would make the difference.

The stars seemed to be no higher than the ceiling of his adobe house on the Texas Colorado. He felt that if he stood up he could pluck one of them right out of the heavens and have for his own a piece of the universe that even now made transitions of day and night, life and death, seem insignificant.

He wanted to sleep more than he had ever wanted anything in his life, but he had to stay awake.

How to stay awake!

Pain, he thought. I'll use pain. Ellis moved so carefully that not even the sand below him was disturbed. He held up his left hand and little by little began to make a fist over the raw palm.

The pain jolted clear up to his elbow and on past to his shoulder. It jarred him and his whole attention was focused on releasing the pressure of the fist and stopping the pain.

At last he opened his hand and he was awake.

There was movement up ahead. He jerked the Colt up and listened.

Ellis had forgotten about his breathing in those few seconds during which he closed his fist. In those seconds the south breeze had carried his position to Goose Face and now the savage made ready to use his knowledge.

He would have to do a reckless thing, but he felt confident now. He released the tension on the bowstring and held the shaft on cock with his forehand around the bow. With his free hand he pulled out his tomahawk and waited again for the breathing, just to make sure.

He heard nothing. Had he been wrong?

There! He heard it again. Without hesitation, Goose Face threw the tomahawk where he thought the foe should be and tensed. The whanged, colored threads of buffalo hide strung to the handle of the weapon whistled through the air. He was ready with the bow, shaft drawn.

The tomahawk landed and he heard the enemy groan, but was it a second late? Did the foe realize that it would be better to make a sound at that moment and seemingly betray his position while staying well hidden?

No, the man had been hit. Goose Face jerked up and threw the arrow.

There was a pure red, then a yellow flash of light to the right of where he had thrown his shaft.

Then something plunged into his body, something hot and fiery that burned his chest. Too late, Goose Face knew he had made a mistake. He had been beaten. But had he taken the white with him? Had the shaft also burned into the chest of the white?

His mouth was full of sand and Goose Face realized that he was screaming and clawing at the red-hot thing that had torn into his chest. He opened his eyes.

The white stood over him. Fuzzily, Goose Face looked for the shaft in the white's body. He saw nothing.

116

The white grabbed his head roughly. Goose Face screamed.

Ellis pulled the hog-sticker from his holster and yanked the hair of Goose Face back away from the forehead. He slit the skin and peeled the scalp back from the white mask, down which tears of anger, hate, fatigue and finality were flowing.

Ellis stood up and looked down at Goose Face's dead body. If he had not seen the white mask a second before he heard the bowstring, Ellis would be the one losing his hair. It had appeared like a bodiless specter against the black sky and Nathan Ellis had fired at it out of sudden, uncontrollable fear — fear of the unknown rather than fear of the savage Cheyenne, Soft-and-Running-Deer, known to the world as Goose Face.

* * *

With the body of Slocum jack-knifed across the back of his horse, Ellis climbed into the saddle and spurred his pony gently. "Let's go, hoss," he whispered.

The animal dug its way out of the gully they had followed earlier and Ellis headed it in the direction of the faint glow on the northeastern horizon of the plains. The blaze of a thousand lanterns and camp fires of the railhead settlement guided him in the moonless night.

The dark, lustrous hair of Goose Face trailed from his stirrup.

Chapter Nine

THERE WERE SECTIONS of the tent community that did not bounce back with brawling jocosity. Amid the ashes were men, women and children, numb to the tragedy that had befallen them. A few had lost everything: family and all worldly goods. But in the grog tents men and women with no responsibilities but to themselves drank and fought and recounted the terror of the stampede and the brutal attack by Goose Face.

The fire had been quickly isolated and stamped out, a good fifth of the camp had been burned.

Jeremy Watson's tents had not been touched. His stock of whisky was intact and at midnight—after the general emergency was over and nothing left to do but bury the dead and clean up the mess—the lanterns were lit and the maw of his big tent opened to the Johnny-Jacks. The weary men pushed and shoved their way to the front of the plank bar and paid four and five dollars a pint for whisky ladled out of the earthen crocks. Side by side, men and women tried to forget the massacre.

* * *

Liza Reeves had ignored medical aid and fought alongside the men during the attack. And when a doctor insisted on looking at her wound, he announced that the cauterizing had effectively sealed the fleshy hole, and, considering the amount of bleeding, was probably clean and would heal with no after-effects.

Liza had turned to the grief-stricken women and children after Goose Face had been driven off. She had helped locate lost children, re-united husbands and wives, helped the prostrate victims of arrow wounds. She had worked without stopping, talking softly, harshly, soothingly, with authority. And underneath all of it, she had wondered if she would see the tall Texan again. Often during that long and hectic night, she had glanced to the south and west for signs of a rider.

* * *

At midnight Kelly had seen the last of the scattered equipment sorted and counted. The salvaged wheels of the Jehus' carts were waiting for frames of new wagons to replace those crushed by the stampede. Rails and cross ties, tools and railroad gear of every sort had been collected, replaced and laid in readiness for the Monday morning push. A special train had been dispatched back to the east with the critically wounded and a message sent ahead to have a supply train loaded and ready to leave on the return trip at daybreak on Sunday morning.

Kelly whipped and bucked, threatened and pleaded, and got the dead-tired men to work cleaning up the railroad gear. A very tired army of Johnny-Jacks would not be paid, Liam Kelly told them, until he was satisfied.

At midnight the men lined up before the general's caboose to collect their money and then dropped into a dead sleep at the first protected spot they could find. Many of them said to hell with sleep and headed for the grog tents.

At midnight the men and women of the Union Pacific Railroad advance camp were emerging from the nightmare.

* * *

Kelly stood still in the middle of a burned-out clearing. He looked around him, his eyes hollow. There must be something else to be done, he thought. Then he stared out to the southwest, wondering if he would ever see

Nathan Ellis again, wondering if the big man, who was not an employee of the U.P. and had drifted into the camp lookin for a man and a fair fight, was now stretched out in the plains grass with a Cheyenne arrow in his back.

He looked around him again. The men had been paid and had dispersed, and even the sudden shrieks of women in pain had ceased to split the air. There was nothing else to be done.

He started for his tent, not at all sure if it had been burned or if his crippled Jehu was still alive, when someone crossed his path and stopped him.

"How do, Kelly."

"Simpson," Kelly growled. "What do you want?"

"I been lookin' for that big cowboy—the one come lookin' for Lefty," replied Watson's man. "Lefty just rode in from Green River with some of the boys. He sent me lookin' for the Texan. Lefty's waitin' at the big tent. That is, if the big'un ain't dead yet—or ain't run out." Simpson snickered.

Kelly replied with a perfectly-timed right hand that sent the man sprawling. Simpson slapped at his Colt. "You shoot me," Kelly growled, "and every Johnny-Jack in this camp will fight to string you up."

Simpson pulled his gun and cocked it. "They won't know who done it, Kelly. I've had enough of you—"

Liza Reeves stepped out of the darkness and chopped the gunman on the back of the head with a tent stake. Simpson rolled over without a sound.

"He wouldn't have shot," Kelly growled, walking over and kicking the gun away.

120

"You don't know a hell of a lot about gunfighters, Mr. Kelly," Liza said. "You look more tired that I feel. I got your Jehu to cookin' some coffee."

Kelly followed Liza Reeves through the scramble of half-burned tenting and erupting luggage. Liza was still wearing the Indian breeches and vest. Her hair was wilder than ever and she had tied a bandanna around here forehead. She looked like a small lithe brave in the darkness.

Over coffee that was thick and hot and sticky-sweet, they sat on the hard ground and stared into the cook fire. The Jehu had lost a good friend in raid. The two of them had come out of New Mexico to work on the railroad and hoped to return with a enough of a stake to buy a spread. Now the boy fought back tears as the dreams vanished.

None of them spoke for a long while. Finally Kelly turned to look in the direction of the laughter coming from Watson's tent. "You think the big fellow will come back, miss?"

"I sure hope he does Mr. Kelly."

"You like the lad, miss?"

"I reckon," Liza said quietly. "He is a pretty good-type fellow."

"I hope," Kelly said, meaning it more than he had meant anything in his life. "I pray, miss, that he'll come back. And if he does, don't let him go after Lefty."

Liza's eyes flashed. "After what we went through today?" She shook her head. "If that man comes back, Mr. Kelly," she said staring into the southwest, "I ain't never goin' to let him out of my sight again. You think I'd let some lowlife gun him down? If I have to hog-tie him and strap him blindfolded to a pony and lead him clear to Yellowstone, hand-feedin' him every step of the way, I wouldn't let him fight no shoot-out."

"He's a head-strong lad, miss."

"That's all right. I reckon I can handle him. Let's just see—" She stopped. "Let's just see if he gets back from chasin' that Injun all over yonder."

"Beans is all we got, Mr. Kelly," the Jehu said apologetically. "I got some hot if you and the lady would like some."

"Bring 'em on, lad," Kelly said. "I'll eat what the young lass can't handle."

"I reckon I could eat a bite or two," Liza said, her eyes on the southwest where it was dark and the south wind blew softly, bringing on its breath the scent of prairie flowers from Texas and Oklahoma.

* * *

At midnight the glow on the horizon grew brighter and Nathan Ellis began to distinguish the flickering of camp fires. His pony was near exhaustion. "Keep goin', hoss," he breathed to the animal and patted its neck. "Both of us goin' to rest soon."

The ride for Nathan Ellis had been a time of reflection. He had faced death many times. As a child he and his infant brother were left with his mother on the banks of the Colorado after his father had been killed by Apaches. Later, as a growing boy, he had fought the southwest Indians himself, and began to range north in search of blood stock for his cattle. Death had been a daily diet during the war when he had snaked the wagon trains up the Santa Fe trail with guns and ammunition brought overland from the Pacific coast. Raids by Indians, white renegades and Union detachments had been common during the drives. He had even gone to the front lines with the Grays to get a taste of real war for six months before he was ordered back to the supply trains.

122

He had no idea how many men he had killed in his life. Certainly there had been more Indians than white men. But Goose Face had been the first the tall Texan had scalped. It was a savage gesture, and an honor only to the Indian.

He glanced down at the blood-caked hair of Goose face, a little white at the edges with war paint, and was glad that he had lifted the hair of the renegade brave. It was a small act indeed by comparison to the devastation Goose Face had brought to the men and women at the camp, but, for what it was worth, his scalp belonged to them.

He guided his pony into the outer edges of the camp, unmindful of the stares and comments of the Johnny-Jacks who began to follow him. The figure of Slocum, with the Cheyenne arrow still imbedded in his skull, and the grimy rider with the raw-red hand and the long black hair of an Indian scalp trailing the dust at his stirrup brought increasing murmurs.

"Is that Goose Face's hair, mister?" one of the Johnny-Jacks asked.

"It sure is," Ellis said.

The news rippled through the crowd. "He got the Injun!"

"There's his hair to prove it!"

"Gimme a drink! Hot damn his red soul to hell!"

Ellis pulled his pony to a stop before Kelly's tent. The big Irishman and Liza Reeves looked up at him from the fire and put the beans to one side.

"Hail Mary, full of grace—" Kelly crossed himself.

Liza Reeves stood up. She pursed her lips and fought back tears. "Well, I see you got your Injun," she managed without breaking down.

"How'd you do it, mister?" The Johnny-Jacks crowded around, examining the scalp Ellis now held in his hand. Others had removed Slocum's body and laid it to rest beneath a blanket.

"I didn't do it," Ellis said. "He done it." He pointed to Slocum. "He killed six of 'em with six bullets."

"And that really is that chile's hair?" a man inquired, standing close to Ellis and looking at the bloody scalp.

"Goose Face is dead," Ellis said. "Only one of his men is still alive."

"But close to a dozen of 'em got away!" somebody shouted.

"Didn't you hear what the man said!" somebody shouted back angrily. "Only one of 'em got away!"

"For sure, it's Goose Face's hair. You can see the smudges of white from the paint he had all over his face." a big Johnny-Jack said loudly.

Kelly got to his feet and, before all of them, embraced Nathan Ellis warmly. "Lad," he said. "I'm glad to see you."

"Goddam, we gotta celebrate!" someone shouted. "Get out the fiddles—"

"But ain't you got no reverence for the dead?" someone else asked.

"Dead, hell I'm glad to be alive!"

The crowd moved away from the tent. Suddenly there came the squeaks of a violin, and then the groans of a concertina filled the air. The men began to form up and stamp the ground and clap their hands, squaring off for the dance. Big, rough Johnny-Jacks, their women and

124

their children joined in the sudden wild release that the death of Goose Face had triggered.

Ellis sat cross-legged on the ground and accepted the coffee the grinning Jehu offered him. Liza Reeves sat at his side.

"How's your leg?" he asked.

"Fair to passin'."

"And your shoulder?"

"Nothin' to trouble about. Here, lemme see that hand of yours." She examined the palm carefully. "Don't reckon you'll be grabbin' at anythin' for a while." She turned to the Jehu. "Gimme some pure grease fat, boy, and one of Mr. Kelly's shirts."

"Ain't no use in doin' that now," Ellis said uncomfortably.

"You just keep your mouth shut," she said tartly. "I reckon if I want to put grease fat on your hand and tie it up in a rag, you ain't goin' to say nothin' about it!" Her eyes flashed at him.

Ellis looked at Kelly.

The big Irishman was busy eating his beans.

* * *

At one-thirty in the morning, his hand bound in the tail of Kelly's nightshirt, Nathan Ellis put coffee down on top of beans and bacon and told them of his man-to-man duel with Goose Face on the plains.

"You rest, lad," Kelly said. "When I tell the general all you've done for his railroad today, he'll show his appreciation in hard money. That's the kind of man the general is. And as soon as you feel able to straddle a horse, you're number-one scout for the Union Pacific Railroad."

"I don't want no job, Kelly," Ellis said. "And I don't want no pay for what I did today. Soon as Lefty shows his face I'll have my showdown and afterwards I'll just cut on back south to the Colorado."

"You ain't gettin' into no gunfight with Lefty, or nobody," Liza said. "So you might just as well get that right clear out of your mind."

"Who said?"

"I said."

"Who do you think you are?"

"Well, you ain't exactly ast me to marry you yet, but you will sometime or other, so I'm just settin' out my fences right now in advance a little bit. You ain't fightin' no professional gun-toter."

"Marry you!"

"Don't act like you don't want to, 'cause it won't get you no place. You ain't goin' to do no more shootin'—leastways not around this camp at Lefty Whatever-his-name-is."

"It wouldn't be wise, lad," Kelly said softly. "Even if you did manage to kill him, I'm sure Watson's men wouldn't let you get away with it."

Ellis sipped his coffee. "As soon as Lefty shows his face, that's when it's goin' to happen."

Liza and Kelly looked at each other quickly, and then were silent. Ellis watched their faces.

"He's in camp, ain't he?"

Liza jumped up. "God damn it! I ain't goin' to let you go!"

Ellis shook his head. "Woman, just stay the hell out of my way."

126

Liza jerked Kelly's Colt out and aimed it at Ellis. "I'll break both of your arms, mister," she said coldly. "You won't be able to lift a gun for six months. If you don't believe me, just try and walk away."

"How come you so interested?" Ellis demanded angrily.

"'Cause I love you, you hard-headed, stubborn Texan!" Liza yelled at him. "I been waitin' a long time for somethin' like you to come along and I ain't goin' to stand by and see you drop in front of the gun of a no-good—"

"Now you listen to me a minute, woman," Ellis said, his voice hard and edged with determination. "I do wantta marry you. And under the circumstances, I guess you'd be right to keep me outa a fight—if it was an ordinary shoot-out—but it ain't."

"What makes this one so different?" Liza demanded.

Ellis pulled out his Colt and began to load it, examining it carefully. He did not look at Kelly or Liza as he spoke. "I got a place down on the Colorado, near Center city, Texas. My paw staked it out forty years ago with my maw. I was born there and worked cattle with my paw. Then my brother was born in the same room as me, six years later.

"Paw was killed in a runnin' fight with some Apaches when they tried to raid the range one night back in fifty-four. The Apaches got our cattle."

Ellis examined each cartridge as he slipped it into the chamber. "Buster, my brother, and me worked the cattle for Maw. We worked up a nice little herd and when beef prices went sky-high back in sixty-one because of the war, we sold off everything except the breed stock. Buster and I came home from the drive that took us halfway across the country—up to Oklahoma so the herd could eat high on the good grass and then on through to the buyers in Missouri—fightin' Indians and raiders, stampedes and cold and rain and heat and drought every step of the way. But we got our price and we went home. Maw said the money was for us—half 'n' half—sixty-eight thousand dollars."

The Colt was loaded and Ellis slipped it back into his holster and stood up. He carefully tied the leather thongs around his thigh and faced Liza. "But the war was on then and I was hot to get in it. I wasn't for the South; I was just against anythin' anywhere at any time. I was a young hard-head wantin' to fight."

The Colt was not quite low enough and he untied the thongs from around his leg and slipped the belt up on his left hip, dropping the Colt another half inch on his right thigh. He began to tie it down again.

"I went off to fight and left Maw and Buster to take care of the breed stock and start buildin' up a really fine herd. Buster was a good breeder and with the money to experiment, we were goin' to have the finest cattle in the country. I got home once in a while to see 'em and every-thin' was fine. We had nearly five hundred head of prime beef—worth about thirty thousand on the markets then—but we didn't want to sell, 'cause that herd was the backbone of the future.

"Then the cattle were rustled and Buster and Maw were killed tryin' to fight the rustlers off. When I got back, I started lookin' for 'em. There wasn't but five of them, and the Indians got two on the trail to market. One of 'em was drowned crossin' the Brazos and the fourth was killed in a saloon in St. Louis spendin' his money. Lefty Hayes was the boss of the outfit and he's the only one left."

Nathan Ellis drew the Colt, testing the position of the butt on his leg. Liza Reeves blinked. Kelly stared in awe at the blur of Ellis' draw.

"So, woman, I'm goin' lookin' for Lefty. I love you and I guess when I get back we'll go on down to the Sky Rock spread on the Colorado—but don't try and stop me now."

He went quickly from the fire into the shadows and headed for Watson's tents.

* * *

The Johnny-Jacks had had their pay just long enough to get good and drunk when Ellis pushed through the maw of the huge tent. He moved toward the bar searching the faces of the men. He did not know Lefty Hayes by sight. His right hand dangled and brushed the butt of the Colt as he toured the bar, stopping now and then to stare at a man who wore his gun slung low, or at the back of another who looked like a rider who might just have returned from Green River. He circled the bar and returned to stand before the huge tent maw.

"By God, here's the fellow that got ol' Goose Face! Have a drink!"

"Give 'im anything he wants, bartender, he's a regular friend of mine!"

"Weeeooooew! Scalped the bastard, he did!"

Ellis accepted the slaps on the back by the working men of the railroad but refused to drink. He put his back to the bar and faced the maw.

Every new arrival was examined by Ellis. Every man who wore a gun was watched expectantly.

"You lookin' for Lefty?" Garrity slipped up quietly beside Ellis.

"You know where he is?"

"He said to tell you he don't even know who you are, and that that word Sky Rock don't mean anythin' to him. But he said if you want a shoot-out, he'll be along in a minute." Garrity backed up. "You goin' to need an extra big grave, mister."

Ellis backhanded Garrity across the face and rammed him up against the bar. Garrity tried to draw his gun. "You draw and I'll blow your guts out," Ellis said harshly.

"What do you want of me? I didn't do nothin'!"

"You go tell Lefty that my name is Nathan Ellis, that he killed my maw and my brother, that I'm goin' to kill him—here—tonight—and that if he rides outa camp I'll trail him for the rest of his life."

Garrity's eyes widened. "Killed your *maw!*"

"Git!" Ellis shoved the man toward the door.

Garrity fled.

The Johnny-Jacks near Ellis had heard everything. They began to fall back quietly.

Watson rounded the corner of the bar and strode up to Ellis. "We don't want no trouble in here. You're disturbin' my business. You got a fight with Lefty, take it outside."

Two of Watson's men stood behind their boss. With his bandaged left hand, Ellis reached for a heavy Johnny-Jack canteen and swung it at Watson's head. He drew the Colt with his right and covered the others.

Watson slumped to the ground "Drop them guns and make it goddam quick!" Ellis commanded.

130

The other two lowered their guns and backed away. Watson groaned and tried to lift his head. Then he opened his eyes and began to crawl away, back from the cleared space before the opening of the tent.

The bar suddenly became silent. A white flag appeared in the mouth of the tent, and Garrity showed himself. "Lefty's coming, big fellow!"

The Johnny-Jacks moved farther back, pressing against the walls of the tent, clearing the space between Ellis and the maw.

There was movement in the shadows beyond the rim of light outside. Ellis tensed.

Liza Reeves, still in her Indian breeches, and Liam Kelly stepped inside. Kelly moved to the one side but Liza strode right up to Ellis. She had Kelly's heavy Colt strapped to her waist. The holster had been tied down.

"Get outa here," Ellis said expressionlessly.

"I reckon I'm goin' to see that it's a fair fight, one way or the other," she said determinedly.

"You'll get killed."

"Mebbe."

"All right, stay then," Ellis said and moved away from her.

There was laughter outside and the sounds of footsteps. Six men wheeled into the tent, Lefty Hayes at the head of them. "What fellow here's goin' to get me for killin' his maw?"

He had hardly finished his words before Liza Reeves had the Colt out and steadied on the six men. "You others just step back with your leather empty."

One of the men laughed and moved for his hip. Liza shot him in the arm. "I said move!"

Ellis had not taken his eyes from Lefty Hayes. Nor had the slight, thin man in dusty trail clothes removed his eyes from Ellis.

Hayes nodded slightly in Liza's direction. "Bring your squaw along to help you fight, boy?"

"Did you rustle five hundred head of cattle from a ranch on the Colorado a couple of years back?"

"Sure I did. What about it?"

"You're my man."

"You callin' me out?"

"You're out."

"Are you woundin' or killin'?"

"One of us goes out in a pine box."

"Make your move, big fellow."

Ellis jerked the Colt out and fanned the hammer five times. Hayes's gun was torn out of his hand by a wild slug. The other four ripped into his chest. Hayes was hurled back to the maw of the tent and hit the ground flat on his back.

Ellis walked over and fired a final bullet into Lefty Hayes's head.

He turned slowly, pushing the Colt into his holster, and motioned to Liza. "Come on," he said.

Liza walked through the clearing, stepped over the body of Lefty Hayes and disappeared into the darkness with Ellis.

Chapter Ten

CAN'T YOU at least stay around until mornin'?" Kelly growled. "You both look like you been dragged through the pit of the damned, and it's only three o'clock now."

"If you don't shut up, Kelly, we're goin' to have that roustin' we started at the railroad train." Ellis grinned. "We got a long way to go. Clear across Kansas and half of Texas before we get home."

"Lad, I'd like to see the two of you married. I'd like to stand up for both of you," Kelly said softly.

"You ain't got a preacher in camp," Liza protested.

"There's a Mexican padre who serves some of the lads on the gang. I don't reckon you belong to the Holy Church, but—"

"I ain't got no objections," Ellis said.

"Me neither," Liza said.

"I'll go get him. Come with me."

"You come, too, boy," Ellis said to the Jehu. "Damned if I don't feel good all of a sudden."

* * *

Their names had been entered on the official log of the railroad and they had signed the sleepy-eyed priest's prayer book. They had been given the finest horses in the railroad's corral, fitted with saddles from the supply house, blankets and a sack of beans, coffee and sugar. The Jehu had miraculously found Ellis's carbine and it had been cleaned and loaded. Mr. and Mrs. Ellis swung to the backs of their ponies and shook hands all around. Kelly was crying unabashedly. "I'll never forget you, lad. Nor you, miss."

"Missus, now," Liza said with a grin.

"We call it the Sky Rock. It's on the Colorado near Center City, Texas, Kelly. That's where we'll be any time you want to visit." Ellis nodded to the Jehu. "Boy, when you get sick of railroadin', you come on down to Texas. We'll help you find a place for yourself."

The Jehu grinned. "Thank you, mister."

"Let's go, woman. We got a lot of travelin' to do before the heat of the day."

They waved to Kelly and turned their horses south and favoring the east a little.

Kelly watched them disappear into the southeastern sky where the sun would emerge soon, and then turned to his tent.

"There's a letter for you, Mr. Kelly," the boy said. "It has a funny-lookin' stamp."

Kelly smiled. His Kathleen had not forgotten. Well, he sighed, pulling off his boots and loosening his belt, I wonder if her sister's caught herself a lad yet.

In the light of a lantern, wire-framed spectacles on the end of his nose, Kelly opened the letter from his wife.

"My dearest," he said, reading aloud. "It is so quiet and peaceful here—I wonder if you are blessed with the same?"

* * *

They had ridden without stopping into the heat of the day, when they struck a stream of running water.

"I reckon we better light and rest," Ellis said, not looking at his wife. "Hungry?"

"I could eat, I reckon," Liza said casually. "You take care of the horses and I'll set to makin' somethin' or other."

134

They camped in the depth of a clump of trees where birds sang. Liza expertly made a fire, put cans of beans against fire, stripped bacon with her knife, and smoked it above the flames.

Ellis returned and squatted down beside the fire. He accepted the can of beans Liza had opened with her knife and bit into a hot strip of bacon.

They ate hungrily and in silence, not looking at each other, speaking in unnaturally casual tones, when they spoke at all, about the raid or Kelly or the crippled Jehu, not really even thinking about what they said.

Liza took a great deal of time putting out the fire. Finally she turned to look at Ellis.

Her eyes widened.

Ellis was advancing toward her, a huge bar of gray soap in his hand. "I've been wantin' to give you a bath since the first time I seen you."

Liza backed off. "Now hold on—"

"You goin' to come gentle, or am I goin' to have to tie you down?"

Liza turned to run, but she had hesitated a moment too long. Ellis grabbed her by the wrist.

"No, you don't!" Liza screamed. "No man's goin' to wash me—"

"I am," Ellis said heavily. He dodged her slashing nails. Slinging her lightly to his shoulder, he carried the screaming, kicking Liza toward the creek.

At the edge of the water Liza bit him on the arm. Ellis bellowed and threw her into the water. She came up gasping. Nathan Ellis grinned and dove in after her.

Off to the side the horses raised their heads at the noise and then went on nuzzling the grass.

135

Photo-History

The text, photographs, and captions in the next section do not represent a complete history of the Transcontinental Railroad. Some content was chosen with *Cheyenne Saturday* in mind. The rest consists of other interesting tidbits about life on the Railroad.

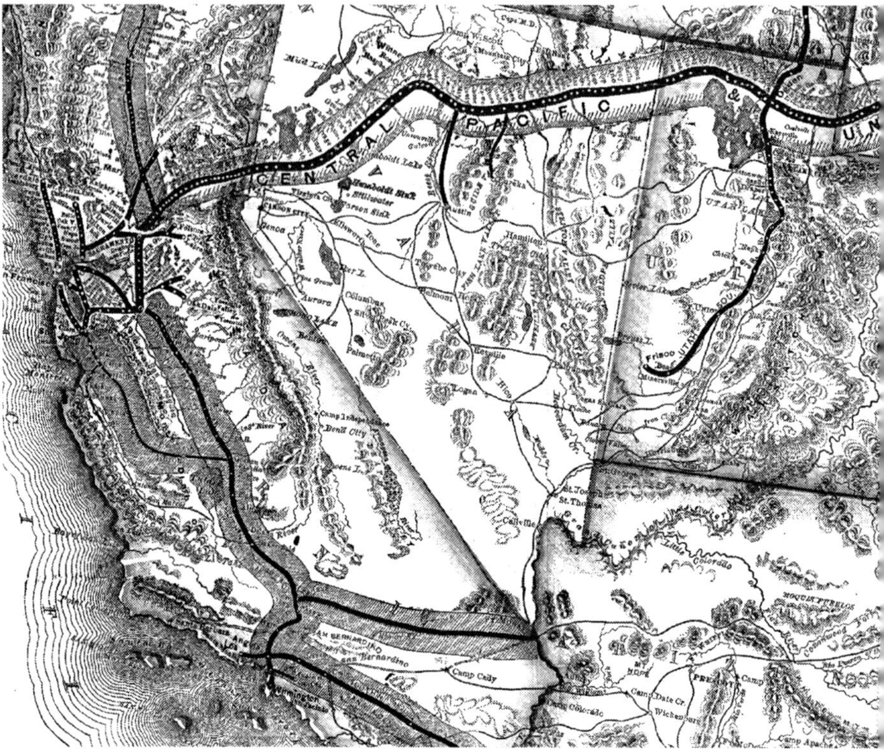
CENTRAL
PACIFIC

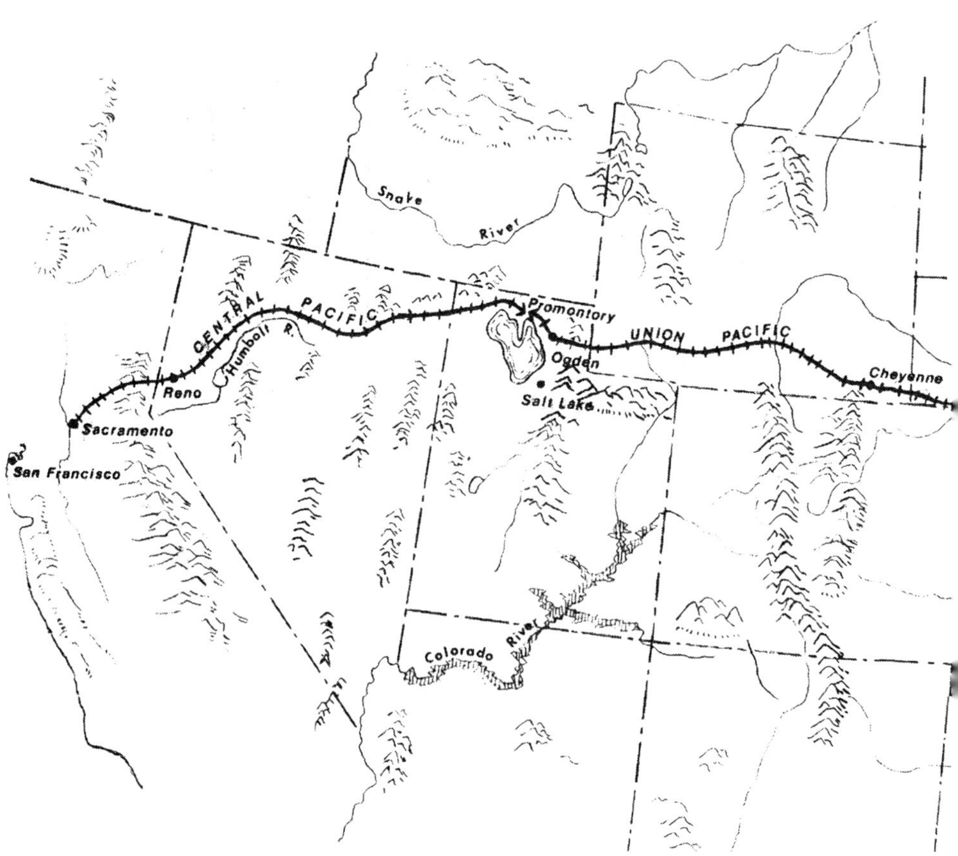
Snake River
CENTRAL PACIFIC
Humbolt R.
Promontory
UNION PACIFIC
Ogden
Salt Lake
Cheyenne
Reno
Sacramento
San Francisco
Colorado River

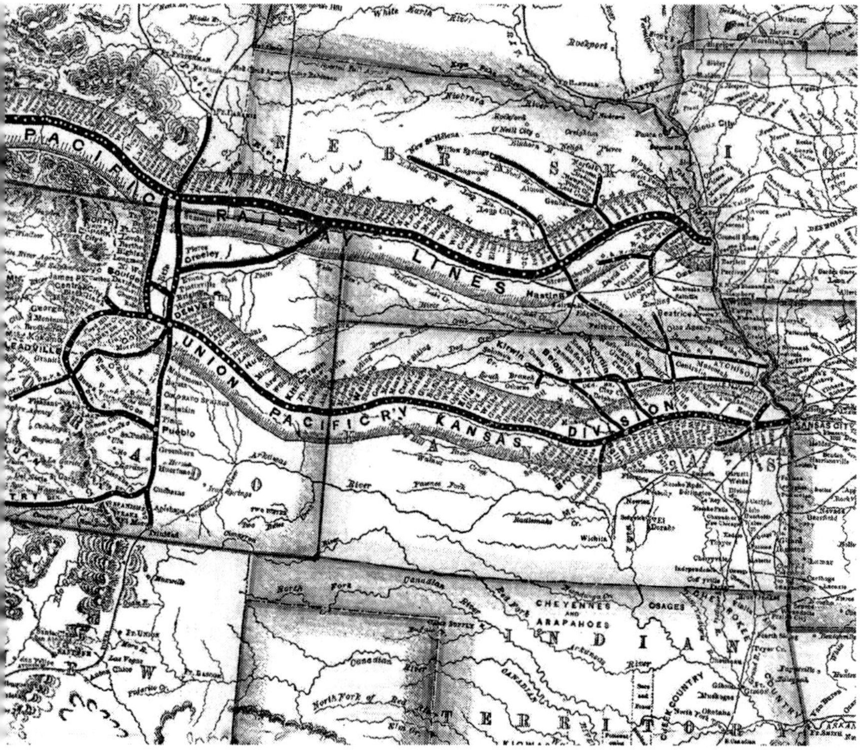

(above) The Rand, McNally 1881 Overland Railroad Connections and 30,000,000 acre Land Grant map. The line consisted of more than 6000 miles of rail--1914 of which were the main line between Omaha and San Francisco. The highest point along the line is in the Rocky Mountains at Sherman--8242 feet above sea level.

(left) The main line showing Promontory, Utah—the convergence point of the Union Pacific Railroad and the Central Pacific Railroad. Cheyenne was roughly halfway between Salt Lake and Omaha and was designated as a division point. People started settling Cheyenne just two days after its creation. The population in 1867 was in the thousands and its popularity brought on the nickname, "the Magic City of the Plains."

Brigadier General Grenville M. Dodge circa 1863. Dodge was designated chief engineer of the Union Pacific Railroad.

(right) Samuel Skerry Montague was chief engineer of the Central Pacific Railroad. He conducted extensive surveys across Nevada and Utah, going as far east as Green River, Wyoming.

General Dodge's words regarding the Indian threat and the deaths of two of his best survey chiefs—Percy T. Brown and L. L. Hills:

> "In the spring of 1867 there was a party in the field under L. L. Hills, running a line east from the base of the Rocky Mountains. The first word I received of it was through the commanding officer at Camp Collins, who had served under me when I commanded the department. He informed me that a young man named J. M. Eddy had brought the party into that post, its chief having been killed in a fight with the Indians. I enquired who Eddy was and was informed that he was an axman in the party, and had served under me in the civil war. . . . The fight in which Mr. Hills, the chief, was killed occurred some six miles east of Cheyenne, and after the leader was lost young Eddy rallied the party and by force of his own character took it into Camp Collins. Of course I immediately promoted him."

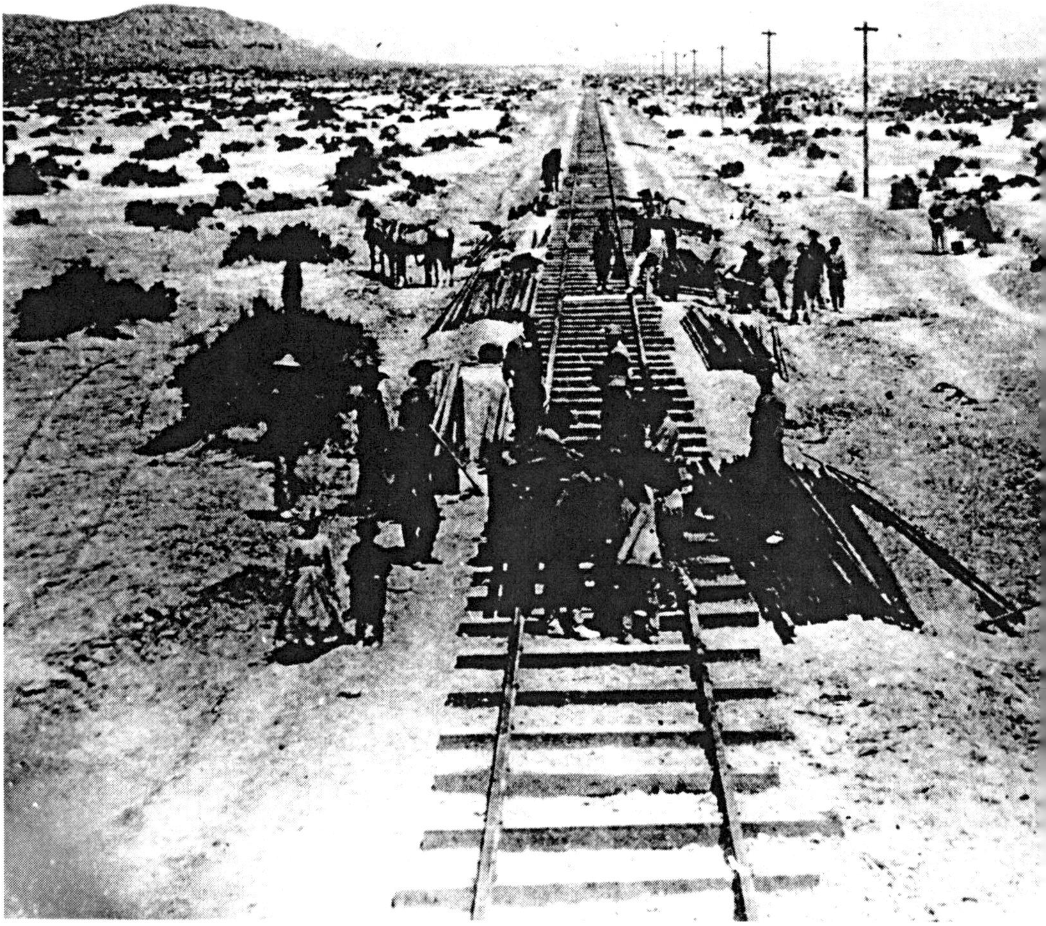

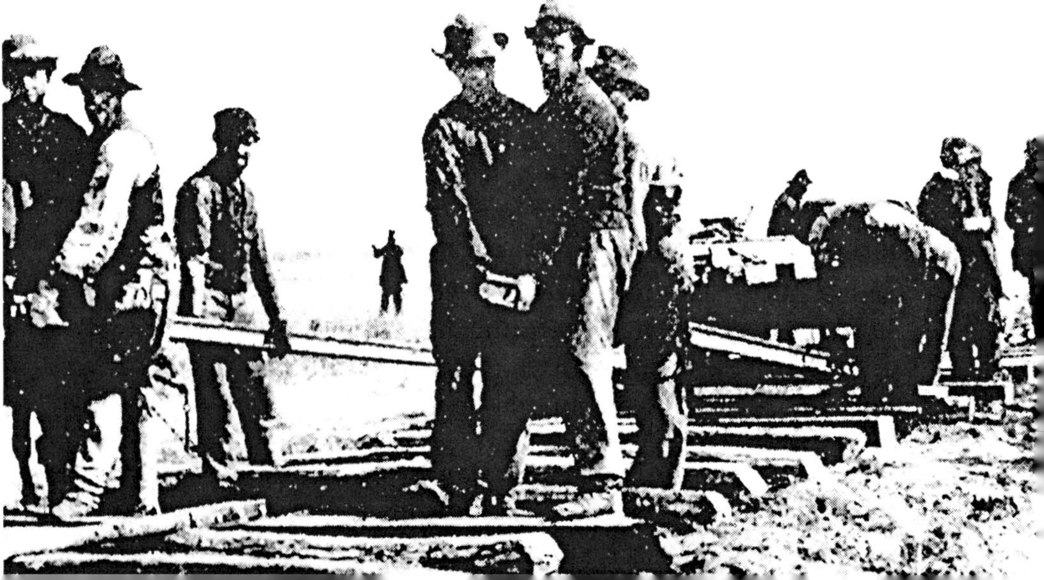

(top) The Central Pacific line running through Green River, Wyoming.

(left-top) Central Pacific workers laying track. Nevada, 1868.

(left-bottom) Central Pacific crew laying track near the Humbolt River. Nevada, 1868.

(top-right) Laborers for the Central Pacific Railroad Company. Chinese immigrants became the prime source of manpower. In 1868, the total number of Chinese that had worked for the railroad was over 12,000—they represented more than 80% of the entire Central Pacific work force.

The Central Pacific Railroad Company experienced a serious labor shortage in 1865. There was enough work for 4000 men but the company had difficulty keeping even 800 workers at a time. The majority of this early work force was made up of Irish immigrants. Prejudices of the day led recruiters to believe the Irish spent all their earnings on liquor and the Chinese were unreliable. Contractors begrudgingly hired fifty Chinese workers to quell a wage dispute in which a large crew of Irish workers threatened to walk out. Those fifty workers proved themselves and sparked a hiring frenzy—job advertisements showed up as far away as the Canton Province, China.

Teams often consisted of twenty Chinese workers and one white foreman, although team size grew for difficult stretches of grading and laying track. Chinese employees earned $30 a month, minus the cost of food and board. The Irish earned $35 a month with board provided at no charge.

(left) Wagon train following behind the builders of the Transcontinental Railroad and responsible for building up settlements along the line.

Crude methods were employed when track had to be curved. The 56 pound yard iron rail, measuring 32 feet in length, was laid across two railroad ties spaced 25 feet apart. Eight workers would stand on the rail as the hammer-man struck with a heavy sledge. The weight of the men provided just enough spring to bend the rail slightly. The position of hammer-man required great skill and strength. They were responsible for measuring the curves by sight and determining where a strike was needed to balance the rail.

Bad weather was a continuing challenge. The winter of 1866 brought forty-four snowstorms, avalanches, and—for the crews tunneling through mountains—the excruciating job of clearing ice and rubble at the entry point. The snow pack at the top of the Sierra Nevadas could reach a depth of eighteen feet. Camp 4, known as Strong's Mountain Camp was hit by a slide that wiped out two gangs of tunnelers working Tunnels 11 and 12 as well as a gang of culvert men. Avalanches aside, camps in these violent weather conditions offered workers little respite from a day on the rail head.

(right) Track gang curving rail in Ten-Mile Canyon along the Humbolt River in Nevada, 1867.

(above) Eadward Muybridge, a prominent English photographer, documented some of the brilliant engineering and displays of brute strength along the Central Pacific line.

Crews of workers drove spikes into the solid granite and used black powder to blast their way through—inch by inch. One of the most impressive feats of engineering was Tunnel 6, which bored its way through the Sierra Nevada Mountains. Four teams stepped up to that task; one at the east and west sides, and one going each way out from the middle—accessible by a vertical shaft. Engineers were so accurate they discovered the tunnel was off by only two inches when the east and west tunnels converged and broke through.

(above) End of the track near Humbolt River Canyon, Nevada, 1868. The Central Pacific campsite and train are at the foot of the mountains.

The first train arrived in Cheyenne in September of 1867 but nearby Laramie—a mere 50 miles away—didn't see the Union Pacific crew come through until May of 1868. Cheyenne was a stopping point for Union Pacific workers as engineers tackled one of the biggest challenges the railroad would face—the Dale Creek Trestle. The winter of 1867-68 was spent constructing what, at the time, was the highest railroad bridge in the world.

The federal government needed to protect the rail, track-layers, and the burgeoning tent towns along the line. Fort Sanders, south of Laramie, was already in existence before the Union Pacific came through. At Cheyenne, though, Fort D.A. Russell was built with the specific purpose of protecting the railroad. The forts provided security from Indian attacks but many of the "hell-on-wheels" towns—an apt nickname for those popping up along the railhead—needed protection from themselves. The first mayor in Laramie stepped down after just three weeks because he saw the town as "ungovernable," leaving law and order to be doled out by vigilantes and through lynchings.

(top) City of Cheyenne, Wyoming, 1876. Showing growth of a tent city along the Transcontinental line.

(bottom) Rock River train depot, Albany County, Wyoming, 1900. Showing growth of one of the stops along the Union Pacific portion of the Transcontinental rail line by Laramie.

Press representatives in an excursion party to 100th meridian, 275 miles west of Omaha, Nebraska, to meet with Eastern capitalists and other prominent figures. October, 1866.

(left-top) Example of an early Central Pacific locomotive for the US Military. Rail transport was critical during the Civil War.

(left-middle) Union Pacific #119. The locomotive that touched noses with Central Pacific's #60 'Jupiter' in Promontory, Utah, at the Golden Spike ceremony.

(left-bottom) Union Pacific directors on the 100th meridian awaiting the arrival of the excursion party of press reps and business men.

Central Pacific's 'Jupiter' (one of the two locomotives in the famous picture three pages ahead) was actually a standby. The initial choice—Diamond Stack #29 'Antelope'—was being towed to the ceremony by Jupiter when log-cutters mistakenly rolled a large log down a hill, striking the Antelope.

The Jupiter was a 4-4-0 steam locomotive built in September, 1868 by Schenectady Locomotive Works. It was then dismantled and sent by river barge to the Central Pacific headquarters in Sacramento. It's inaugural run was March 20th, 1869.

Eight Irish track layers—Michael Shay, Patrick Joyce, Michael Kennedy, Thomas Dailey, George Wyatt, Michael Sullivan, Edward Kieleen, and Fred McNamara—stepped up to the challenge laid out by the boastful Central Pacific promoter, Charlie Crocker. That seemingly impossible goal was to complete the railroad's last 700 mile advance to Promontory, Utah by laying ten miles of track in a single day. Two years earlier the crew would have been lucky to put one mile down a day. Years of constant laying, though, had transformed the process into a near exact science.

On April 28th, 1869, sixteen cars of material—bolts, rails, spikes— were unloaded in eight minutes. The hardware was piled onto small railcars by six-man teams and then each car was pulled up the line by two horses and unloaded by crews of Chinese laborers. Three men aligned the wood ties to the surveyor stakes. The work was then on the backs of the eight Irish track layers—who set out each rail, hammered the eight spikes, and bolted the fishplate at the joint. Behind them, levellers lifted ties and shoveled dirt under to ensure the track was level. The gang laid 144 feet of track a minute. 3,524 rails, 28,160 spikes, 25,800 ties and 12 hours later the job was done. Each of the men had hefted 1800 rails; the eight men combined had moved two million pounds of track in half a day.

Surprisingly, the ceremony to drive the last spike (photo on next page) was not supposed to take place when and where it did. The Union Pacific and Central Pacific were racing to lay the most rail and, as a result, they converged in the undesirable Promontory, Utah, at a time when the promoters, key businessmen, and government officials could not attend the event.

On May 10th, 1869, Leland Stanford of the Central Pacific and Union Pacific's Thomas Durant each awkwardly swung the ceremonial hammer at the last spike—and missed. Two swings later the two groups performed a champagne toast in front of their representative locomotives—the #119 from Union Pacific and Central Pacific's #60 Jupiter. Contrary to popular belief, the last "golden" spike was actually one of five that day, and the only spike that was actually driven into the tie was of the plain iron variety. The other four spikes—two solid gold, one solid silver, and one made of iron with silver on the shaft and gold plating on the head—were temporarily placed into pre-drilled holes in a laurelwood tie that was later cut up and distributed to important figures in business and the government. All five spikes currently reside in museums around the country.

151

Biography

Richard Jessup (01/01/1925 – 10/27/1982) was born in Savannah, Georgia and died in Nokomis, Florida. He lived in and out of orphanages until age sixteen – when he ran away to join the United States Merchant Marine. In eleven years of seamanship, he claimed he read a book a day and learned to write by typing out the complete text of *War and Peace* and editing out the errors – he subsequently threw the edited work in the ocean. Jessup was married to Vera in 1944 and had a daughter named Marina. He left the Merchant Marine in 1948 to become a fulltime author. He was at the typewriter ten hours a day.

His first novel, *The Cunning and the Haunted*, was published in 1954 and filmed as *The Young Don't Cry* in 1957. Three other novels were also adapted to film – *The Deadly Duo*, *Chuka*, and *The Cincinnati Kid*. He sold the movie rights to the 1971 novel *Foxway* but it was never filmed. Jessup published eleven novels – primarily westerns and spy thrillers – as Richard Telfair. His last novel, *Threat*, was published in 1981.

Jessup's obituary claims he wrote under multiple pseudonyms and published over sixty novels. At this time we can only confirm the pseudonym Richard Telfair and the existence of thirty-four published novels.

Bibliography

Written as Richard Jessup

1954 – The Cunning and the Haunted (The Young Don't Cry)
1955 – A Rage to Die
1956 – Cry Passion
1957 – Cheyenne Saturday
1957 – Comanche Vengeance
1958 – Long Ride West
1958 – Lowdown
1958 – Texas Outlaw
1959 – The Deadly Duo
1959 – The Man in Charge
1960 – Sabadilla
1960 – Night Boat to Paris
1961 – Chuka
1961 – Port Angelique
1961 – Wolf Cop
1963 – The Cincinnati Kid
1967 – The Recreation Hall
1969 – Sailor
1970 – A Quiet Voyage Home
1971 – Foxway
1974 – The Hot Blue Sea
1981 – Threat

Written as Richard Telfair

1958 – Day of the Gun
1958 – Wyoming Jones
1959 – The Bloody Medallion
1959 – The Corpse that Talked
1959 – The Secret of Apache Canyon
1959 – Wyoming Jones for Hire
1960 – Scream Bloody Murder
1960 – Sundance
1961 – Good Luck, Sucker
1961 –The Slavers
1962 – Target for Tonight

Film Adaptations
1957 – The Young Don't Cry
1962 – Deadly Duo
1965 – The Cincinnati Kid
1967 - Chuka

Other Empty-Grave Releases
(As of November 2011)

Richard Jessup
The Cincinnati Kid - Tango Edition
CHUKA - Vanilla Edition

Richard Jessup writing as Richard Telfair
The Bloody Medallion - Vanilla Edition

CPSIA information can be obtained at www.ICGtesting.com
Printed in the USA
BVOW011007210513

321283BV00018B/397/P